Mr. Mona Lisa

Balestier Press
Centurion House, London TW18 4AX
www.balestier.com

Mr. Mona Lisa

A CIP catalogue record for this book is available from the British Library.

ISBN 978 1 913891 12 5

Cover design by Rob Janoff
Illustration by Bunsom Chhorn

This book is a work of fiction. The literary perceptions and
insights are based on experience; all names, characters, places,
and incidents either are products of the author's imagination
or are used fictitiously.

MR. MONA LISA

A novel by

Arlene Jaffe

BALESTIER PRESS
LONDON · SINGAPORE

"Time stays long enough for anyone who will use it."

—Leonardo DaVinci

Rob Janoff and I have known each other for a long time.
Half a lifetime to be exact.
First, as an art director/copywriter creative team for
clients from Granny Goose potato chips and Intel chips
to the early days of Apple Computer.
Since he designed one of the world's most iconic logos,
Rob has become sort of an icon himself.
But Rob is still Rob to me.
With years of true friendship forged in the longevity
of distance, closeness, moving, marriage, divorce,
birth, death, illness, wellness, low points, high praise,
misspent youth and grown-up excess.
How time flies when you're with a friend like Rob Janoff.
I thank him for the cover design of Mr. Mona Lisa.
The book you now hold in your hand.

The book I now dedicate to Rob.

Arlene Jaffe
October, 2021

MR. MONA LISA

A STORY (NOT HISTORY) THAT DIDN'T HAPPEN
BUT IT COULD HAVE

BY ARLENE JAFFE

To - Naomi -
Thanks for taking care
of me - Arlene Jaffe
5/512-20222

IN 1503, PEOPLE ARE GOING ABOUT THEIR RENAISSANCE business on the northeastern side of the Piazza Santissima Annunziata near the city center of Florence.

Suddenly, everyone's distracted.

Young women are pointing. Old women knowingly smile at one another. Young and old men alike are practically breathless at seeing the man they had always hoped to see.

Is it him? The revered union boss?

He certainly looks rich, charismatic, and self-absorbed enough dressed in the most elegant and opulent earth-toned layers of silk, satin and wool money can buy.

With a flourish, he smooths his waistcoat that was adorned with intricately looped bouclé.

With a tease, he adjusts his elegantly tailored breeches.

With a hint of annoyance, he removes a piece of gravel from his cape woven with threads of real gold that shimmer under the Tuscan sun.

Mesmerized, the people watch him walk through the Piazza like he owns the place, with the same strut adopted 500 years later by Tony Manero in *Saturday Night Fever*.

It's good to be Francesco Giocondo.

He continues the swagger, acknowledging the admiration of many onlookers on the way to his destination: The Basilica della Santissima Annunziata. The closer Giocondo gets to the steps of the basilica, the more confident (if that's possible) he becomes. When he finally reaches the basilica steps, a voluptuous young woman blows him a kiss. He licks his lips in return, then bounds up the steps to the wooden door of the church.

The exterior, with just a few plain arches and columns, seems unimpressive.

But behind the edifice lies a holy complex of building after building surrounded by rows and rows of white Lilium candidum, the pure and delicate Madonna lily.

The interior is a jaw-dropping majesty sumptuous as the renowned cathedrals of Rome.

The windows, the frescos the statues.

And in the entrance, a painting of the Annunciation for which the basilica is named, which has been proudly displayed there since the thirteenth century.

IN 1252, THE SEVEN ORIGINAL MEMBERS OF THE SERVITE Order founded The Basilica della Santissima Annunziata. These monks have a painfully deep devotion to the Virgin Mary and the glorious depths of her suffering. They exist to serve only her.

Dressed in coarse, black robes with a cowl, hood, and waist rope, four of these monks were gathered in a plain room hundreds of years before the basilica went glam. Precariously perched on old wobbly boxes, they sit quietly at a long, worn table strewn with raw artist materials.

In various stages of organization and clean up, the monks carefully measure mineral pigments in red and yellow ochre, umber, and lime from bowls into storage jars. They proceed to mix the leftover pigments with water and fresh eggs for a viable, pliable tempera paint.

Monk #1; "Young Bartolomeo has been working on the painting for months. And months".

Monk #2: "He doesn't eat, he doesn't sleep."

Monk #3: "It seems our prayers for him are not enough. Neither is our paint. Even this ultramarine I made from ground lapis lazuli." He holds up the intense blue paint. "Bartolomeo said it was to color her mantle. Deep as the sky at midnight."

Monk #4 gingerly picks up a delicate sheet of gold-leaf. "Don't forget real gold to crown our Holy Queen. And to paint Gabriel's halo."

Monk #1: "Yes, he is a novice. But we chose Bartolomeo because he is blessed with God-given talent. With grace and humility, he has accepted our unanimous choice."

Monk #4: "Indeed, the most qualified artist among us."

Monk #2: "Yet who among us could ever do justice to the moment when Gabriel tells Mary she is the Immaculate Virgin."

Monk #4: "The Blessed Mother of God."

Monk #3: "Holy Lady of Mercy."

Monk #1: "Our Queen of Peace."

Monk #5 enters. He carries a loaf of bread in a basket. "This is the brown bread I baked for Bartolomeo to honor Mary, our Morning Star. Yet he was *non grates*. Not interested."

Monk #6 enters, carrying a platter of delicious-looking fish. "He also rejected the trout I cooked for him. Made with almonds that signify the purity of the Virgin."

Monk #3: "He turned down loaves and fishes?"

Monk #5: "Sadly, yes."

Monk #7 enters, holding a wooden goblet he's trying not to spill. "Who could say no to Amarone wine with grapes I pressed myself? Bartolomeo could say no. And he did." The monk proceeds to drink the wine himself.

Monk #5: "When I brought the bread, I saw Bartolomeo standing in front of the painting, shaking his head again and again and again. I fear our brother is never going to finish."

Monk #6: "Worse, I fear he is going mad."

One of the monks begins to chant in Latin. The Gregorian Hymn to the Blessed Mother of God: the somber, moving, and exquisite Ave Maria, Hail Mary. The other monks join in.

THEIR CHANTING FADES AS HE MOVES FURTHER AWAY from the monks. Inside a room with haphazard sketches on the walls, Bartolomeo wears torn, paint-splattered clothing. Looking to the heavens through a small window, he holds a paintbrush in his right hand like a dead weight.

The sun is setting. Bartolomeo drops the paintbrush on the floor littered with broken brushes, empty bowls of pigment and dried paint. In one corner of his "studio," there is a pile of rags topped with straw and covered with a threadbare blanket. This is Bartolomeo's bed.

He paces the entire room. Back and forth around the perimeter. Sweating. Weeping. Again at the window, Bartolomeo screams aloud for everyone and no one to hear.

"Shame! Shame! Shame descends upon me, and I am ashamed." He pounds the window frame three times, then walks from the window toward the longest, furthest wall.

Shaking his head, Bartolomeo now stands in front of his Annunciation painting: a very large horizontal panel of heavy poplar leaning against a bare wall. It is covered with a crumpled canvas tarp. He lovingly touches the left side of the painting, then gently pulls down the tarp to reveal a bit of angel Gabriel.

Bartolomeo repeats from the bible: 'And the angel came in unto her and said, Hail, thou art highly favoured, the Lord is with thee: blessed art thou among women.'

"Luke 1:26 28 didn't say thou art is blessed and highly favoured. But that's how I've continued to behave and should be painfully punished for it. Deservedly. Brutally. Mercilessly punished. For my pride."

Bartolomeo falls to his knees. "Pride is the root of all evil, the deadliest of sins. My pride has multiplied out of all proportion. Arrogance. Hubris." The sky darkens. "For nearly a year, I felt superior, unstoppable, that my talent was far beyond that of ordinary mortals. I felt above my brothers who had chosen me. I witnessed myself become grotesque. A false god. Until this."

Bartolomeo stands like he's a hundred years old. He pulls down the entire tarp. Surprisingly, the painting is nearly complete. But the most glaring omission is that Mary has no face. There is only an empty oval covered with white gesso primer that's yet to be painted.

"Hail Mary. Hail Mary. Hail Mary. Hail Mary. Four times. Forty. Four thousand times."

"I will do penance for the rest of my life should I deserve the rest of my life. Unworthy. Undone. I could never paint a face of such saintly beauty. Capture her expression or even assume to know what that expression might be. Surprise? Fear? Confusion? Distress? Disbelief? Would her eyes weep? Would her brows raise? Would her mouth drop open? Would she smile?"

"If only Mother Mary would come to me in my hour of

darkness and whisper words of wisdom. If only she would forgive me."

Slowly, Bartolomeo drags himself toward the bed, lays down and finally falls asleep in total darkness. He tosses and turns as if trapped in a nightmare on a hellfire sea.

It is dawn of the next day. Bartolomeo is stirred by morning light through the window. He sits up and experiences a violent coughing fit. He rubs his eyes and looks toward the painting.

He rubs his eyes more forcefully, looks at the painting again and wildly jumps up. "Miracle! Mater Dei, it's a miracle." The Annunciation is complete. <u>Mary's face is stunning</u>.

Yelling at the top of his lungs, Bartolomeo runs outside his studio. One by one, the monks, fearing the worst, come running towards him.

"The painting! The painting! Look at the painting!" screams Bartolomeo.

He directs the monks to see what has transpired. As sunbeams highlight the beatific expression on Mary's face, an incredulous Bartolomeo points to the painting, "Last night, unfinished. This morning, complete. No, brothers. Not by my brush, it is the miraculous work of an angel." The monks, simultaneously elated and relieved, applaud and cheer.

Monk #3 kindly asks, "How do you feel at this moment, Brother Bartolomeo?"

"Hungry for trout with almonds, brown bread and Amarone." Rejoicing continues.

In centuries to come, the Servite Order grew to become the holy pioneers of crowdfunding. They built imposing convents and churches, their most famous being the Annunziata in Florence.

Back to Rennaisance rockstar Francesco Giocondo. Now standing directly in front of the basilica door, he bows his head, then looks up to the heavens and crosses himself. Next?

Giocondo takes a deep breath, puts both forefingers in his mouth, tucks his lips over his teeth, closes his mouth around the two fingers and releases a whistle loud enough to not only pierce the northeastern side of the Piazza Santissima Annunziata, but also intense enough to hail a cab in the middle of Times Square.

The heavy door opens. Giocondo walks inside.

A monk stands inside the front door like a Servite sentry. He still wears a black hooded robe like his 13th century predecessors, modernized with the addition of a snazzy leather belt.

Giocondo enters the basilica and greets the monk with a head nod. The monk nods back. Giocondo tries to walk past the monk away from the door. The monk puts up his hand to stop him. Giocondo ignores the monk and proceeds. The monk steps in front of him.

Giocondo replies respectfully "Excuse me, padre." The monk, who is all-gesture-no-talk, nods his head. Giocondo responds less respectfully. "Do you know who I am?" The monk slowly shakes his head.

"I am Francesco Giocondo. G-i-o-c-o-n-d-o. Giocondo like the family who has a private chapel here by the Great Hall. Giocondo who spends money and more money on basilica beautification. Decades of transforming your basilica." The monk puts his palms together as if to give thanks.

"But I am not here to pray in the private Giocondo chapel. I am here for another reason. To see DaVinci." The monk shrugs his shoulders.

Giocondo says, "Leonardo DaVinci. The Last Supper DaVinci. Does that ring a church bell? I have it on the highest authority the maestro has taken residence here. Or should I say given residence here. With a fully paid, very generous patronage that also includes an office, studio, workshop, storage facility, three assistants and a vegetarian cook."

The monk adjusts his leather belt to gird himself, then subsequently, ends his vow of silence.

"God is the highest authority, Mr. Giocondo. And He has advised us if a Mr. DaVinci did reside in Our Lady's house, he is not to be disturbed by outliers."

Giocondo pretends to turn around toward the heavy door.

"You understand, padre, it is the outliers who house you, feed you, and tend to your flock like good shepherds with very deep pockets." He turns around and gets in the monk's face.

The monk knows he's between a rock and an altarpiece.

There is a long face off. The monk blinks.

"Down the southeast hallway past the burial vault and around the corner, you will see a large, vertical frame that's empty. It will appear, Mr. Giocondo, that a painting has been taken out of the frame either for repair or for reconstruction."

"An empty frame, you say."

"An empty frame that isn't really a frame."

Giocondo is getting exasperated. "What is it really."

"A door. Proceed through the door to an unmarked hallway running parallel to a courtyard much smaller than all the other courtyards. You will see another empty frame."

Giocondo is running out of patience. "Another door."

The monk nods his head. "Proceed southeast down a set of circular stairs which have seen better days. At the bottom of the staircase, The Virgin Mary will guide you to your destination."

The monk points southeast. Giocondo hurries in that direction. On the way, he passes Bartolomeo's painting of the Annunciation without a second glance.

GIOCONDO STANDS OUTSIDE THE SEMI-OPEN DOOR OF AN office/library. He quietly pushes the door open to peer inside. He sees an older man with coiffed, cascading, reddish-grey hair and beard.

The man sits on a wooden stool at a huge drafting table. Wearing a pale pink velvet tunic, an even snazzier belt and soft purple cap, he sketches in a leather notebook with his left hand.

There is a tall bookcase against one wall and shelves above the table filled with bound books and hundreds of leather notebooks of various sizes. A wealth of drawing supplies sits on the table, from pens and inks to sticks of black charcoal, colored chalks and papers galore.

The man is Leonardo DaVinci. Without ever turning around, he asks, "Are you lost?"

Giocondo responds with confidence. "I know this basilica like the back of my hand."

DaVinci, still not turning around, asks, "Are you a monk?"

Giocondo replies, "Do I look like a monk?"

DaVinci turns around and answers, "Perhaps from the

Order of the Noble Peacock."

From a strategically placed pocket in the lining of his cape, Giocondo removes a letter.

"This is a letter of introduction, addressed to you, Maestro. It is from the Pope. Personally."

Giocondo offers the letter to DaVinci. He stands up, walks a few steps toward Giocondo, takes the letter, sees the Papal seal, reads the letter and says, "Mr. Giocondo. Please put this letter into the ornate wooden box at the end of this table." DaVinci gestures to the box location.

Of course, Giocondo does exactly what is asked of him. He puts the letter on top of a towering pile of other letters that look surprisingly similar. "This towering pile of letters. They are all letters...introductory letters...written in the pope's hand...just like the one I brought to you?"

"Yes, and it seems you all desire the same thing." DaVinci sits back down to sketch.

"I don't think so." Giocondo takes something smaller from another pocket in his cape.

"This is my calling card."

He puts the heavy paper card on the table next to DaVinci's notebook. DaVinci picks it up, turns it over, turns it over again, and puts it down.

"Please, Mr. Giocondo." DaVinci pulls out another wooden stool. "Have a seat."

Giocondo quickly moves the wooden stool close to DaVinci, smiles and sits down. DaVinci picks up the calling card with his left hand, then looks through an ornate magnifying glass with his right. "Excellent work. Perfect alignment. A job well done."

Giocondo is bursting with pride and joy. "The front of my card displays the historical emblem of one of the major guilds in Florence, the wool guild."

This is a four color, beautifully rendered visual of a young, pre-shorn lamb surrounded by a wreath of pinecones and apples.

"On the back," Giocondo continues, "is another famous emblem, that of the silk weavers."

This visual is of a bronze door within a bronze circle. Oddly enough, not at all silk-like.

"I," Giocondo continues, "not to be boastful, am the power behind these major guilds, achieving mercantile domination across Europe and far beyond. As well as the largest employer in all of Florence."

He takes the cuff of DaVinci's tunic between his fingers, manipulating the cloth while speaking. "The finest loop of silk velvet has a wonderful sheen and amazing depth of color. Light reflects off the various angles, so the appearance changes as it drapes and folds."

DaVinci, unimpressed, takes his cuff back and says, "Arte della Calimala guild, Arte della Lana guild, Arte della Seta guild...yada yada yada. There seems to be a miscommunication, Sir."

DaVinci continues. "My comment about excellent work was in reference to the printing quality of your calling card, not the prestige of your guilds. Excellent because Mr. Giunti contacted me directly to help retrofit his operation."

Giocondo is surprised. "Giunti who controls every Italian printing project. That Mr. Giunti?"

"Yes. I improved the function of his entire printing press empire for greater efficiency. It is now an automatic system that moves the type-saddle forward and back along a tilted surface. Gotta love a lever. That's why I said, 'you with your letters from the Pope desire the same thing'.

I can only extrapolate that you, Mr. Giocondo, came here to ask for my help; to make some or all of your manufacturing processes more efficient. And more profitable. Corretto?"

"No. Not corretto. I want you to paint a portrait."

DaVinci is puzzled. "A portrait. Of whom?"

Giocondo is blasé. "Of me, of course."

DAVINCI AND GIOCONDO ARE NOW IN A DIFFERENT, YET connected space. This is DaVinci's studio. Windows overlook a small courtyard, so there is more light here than in his office/library. Tonnage of props, clothing, and military paraphernalia like swords and armor are categorized and organized.

DaVinci sits on a wooden stool with a cushioned seat. Giocondo sits on a chair with a low back, a few feet across from him. Uninstructed, Giocondo strikes a myriad of self- important poses. DaVinci is drawing in a much larger notebook.

"Will that notebook be full of me?" Giocondo asks.

"This notebook is called a codex, Mr. Giocondo. And it will be full of you as you are full of it. Please sit still."

"Sorry, Maestro. Movers and shakers never sit still."

"Perhaps if you remove that heavy cape, you will be more comfortable." DaVinci suggests.

Giocondo stands, removes his cape, drapes it over the back of his chair and sits down. "I am more comfortable discussing business details. Like a contract for compensation and timing."

DaVinci, still sketching, quietly responds. "No contract necessary. My compensation is discussed only when I finish a project. Precisely when that project is finished is determined by me and only me. Solo. Now. Please try on a hat of your choosing from my extensive collection."

Frustrated, Giocondo walks to a wealth of hats on a table in the corner. He chooses the only crown in the bunch, walks back to his chair, sits down, tries on the crown, and poses royally.

"Perfect fit, don't you think, Maestro?"

DaVinci continues sketching. "You realize, Mr. Giocondo, a portrait could take as long to paint as The Last Supper. Three years, give and take."

Giocondo isn't convinced. "You painted twelve apostles on a wall in a sacristy. My portrait, although impressive, should be finished in a matter of weeks, give and take."

DaVinci stops sketching. "You forgot Jesus, Mr. Giocondo. A very unwise omission. However, if you truly want a portrait painted in weeks, I suggest you contact Raphael."

Giocondo crosses his legs, uncrosses his legs, leans back, leans forward, twists his body one way, then the other way, stands up, sits down and yawns.

"If I may be completely honest with you, Mr. Giocondo, portraits hold the least appeal. Every brushstroke consumes me. Lately, my right hand has been a bit uncooperative."

"You're drawing with your left hand." Giocondo points out.

"I paint with my right hand." DaVinci explains.

Giocondo removes the crown. "By the way, on returning from the Coronation of Louis XII,

I stopped in Milan for a meeting with the duke. After which, we decided to view The Last Supper."

Giocondo continues. "I don't think Judas looks like a betrayer."

"What does a betrayer look like, Mr. Giocondo?" DaVinci asks.

"Not like your Judas, Maestro," responds Giocondo.

"Did you see him spill the salt?" asks DaVinci.

"What does that have to do with betrayal?" Giocondo wonders.

"Everything," DaVinci says, strongly,

DaVinci stops sketching, closes the codex and puts it on the floor next to him. He removes his cap, smooths his hair and strokes his beard. "Every portrait I choose to paint is of someone with a secret. Or a longing. Or fighting an inner turmoil buried deep within."

Giocondo goes to the military paraphernalia, picks a helmet and a chest plate. He removes his waistcoat, puts on the chest plate, the helmet and sits to pose, soldier-like. "I am someone with no turmoil buried deep within. I fight in the open where everyone can see me emerge victorious."

"I meant no insult, Mr. Giocondo. But in portraiture, the subject must sit for hours at a time—for weeks or months unmoving. You attend meetings of the highest echelon, you travel from country to country, how can I paint your portrait with a schedule like that?"

Slowly, Giocondo takes off the chest plate and helmet, then puts his regular clothes back on. "What if I could offer something else of value along with a handsome payment. Sweeten the pot as they say. You wouldn't even have to paint my portrait."

"I have no idea of what you are speaking, Mr. Giocondo."

"You're a genius, Maestro. Figure it out." Giocondo says.

"I will," promises DaVinci. "If only you'd stop calling me Maestro."

Giocondo bows to DaVinci, smiles and leaves. DaVinci picks up his codex and opens it.

Inside is a fully-realized drawing of a horse's ass.

GIOCONDO ENTERS THE FOYER OF HIS OWN HOME, THEN walks through the expansive living spaces. There is evidence of packing up the premises: ornate trunks filled with clothing, furniture covered with blankets, cabinets empty but for a few glasses and plates, many empty baskets, etc.

He takes off his cape and looks around. "Lisa. I have wonderful news!" Louder. "Where are you?" Muttering aloud to himself, "I know where you are. Where you always are."

Giocondo bounds up an impressive staircase, walks down a hallway and stops in front of a small room painted pink. He hears a music box playing softly.

Inside is a nursery where nothing has been packed up or slightly disturbed in any way. The lovely crib is intact. There are stuffed animals and toys, mainly little lambs and larger sheep, all around the room. Small, delicate, handmade birds dangle from the ceiling on colorful ribbons.

Lisa, Giocondo's younger wife, is tenderly folding baby clothes. She is a classic Italian beauty in an understated way. Wavy dark hair, unblemished olive skin, womanly body, plainly dressed. She's obviously been crying. Lisa barely looks up as Giocondo walks into the room.

"You're home early, Francesco."

"You're supposed to be packing up this room, Lisa. We're moving in a few days."

She responds, plaintively, "I don't want to move. The memories are here."

"Well, my unfortunate wife, that ship has sailed. Our new address is Medici-adjacent near the Riccardi Palace. This is a house - that is a mansion. More room for more children."

Lisa is emphatic. "We will have no more children."

"Give me your explanation why, Lisa," Giocondo asks her with malice.

Lisa whispers, "You know why. Our healthy baby daughter died in that crib."

Giocondo walks to the crib and violently shoves it against the wall. Lisa jumps up. Frightened yet emboldened, she slowly moves the crib back to its original place.

Emotionless, Giocondo says, "We are moving out and moving on. Weeks of mourning is long enough for anyone, Lisa."

"You were not her mother. "You don't understand. Your heart is ice."

"Ice? My heart beats only for you. I can prove it. Guess who I am engaging to paint your portrait." Silence. "No guesses? How about Leonardo DaVinci." Silence. "DaVinci is the most famous artist in the world. If you don't know, he painted The Last"

She cuts him off mid sentence. "I grew up in the countryside with my three brothers and three sisters. But we didn't live in a barn locked away from civilization. Or art history. And why would he bother painting a portrait of me?"

"You are the wife of Francesco Giocondo. La Gioconda. A noblewoman. A noble woman.

I want your DaVinci portrait to be the first thing anyone sees entering our new home."

Lisa starts folding more baby clothes. Without looking at her husband, she quietly responds.

"No."

A FEW WEEKS LATER, GIOCONDO HAS RETURNED TO DaVinci's office/library. He is winded from the arduous, circuitous route taken for the second time from the front door of the basilica. He is dressed head-to-toe in another iteration of his peacockish best.

Wearing a lavender tunic with a smaller leather belt and a pinkish cap, DaVinci sketches in a different large codex. DaVinci asks, "Why so out of breath, Mr. Giocondo? Not running from international creditors, I hope."

Giocondo says, "I can't believe you walk up and down that dangerous staircase everyday."

DaVinci puts down the large codex, then attaches a much smaller codex to his belt. He walks toward the tall bookcase and rubs his hands together. "I don't." DaVinci pushes the bookcase open to reveal it's actually the door to a small courtyard. "After you, Mr. Giocondo."

IN THE COURTYARD ARE TREES, FLOWERS, A TABLE, CHAIRS, a birdbath and a statue of Mary. The men sit on a bench. DaVinci unhooks the codex from his belt and sketches like the wind...page after page.

"I assume you invented that belt contraption," Giocondo comments. DaVinci nods his head. "Brilliant," Giocondo comments sincerely. "What's not brilliant is a door that lets anybody just stroll right into your private space."

DaVinci shakes his head. "Security, Mr. Giocondo."

Giocondo looks around. "I don't see any security."

"DaVinci explains. "To paraphrase my friend Niccolò Machievelli: 'It is a common fault not to reckon on storms in fair weather. You must, with all stealth and foresight, establish restraints of men who will seize the property of others.' Which is more effective when I can keep it on the down low. But you have not come back to discuss security, Mr. Giocondo. Or have you."

"If we're talking the security of marriage, I have indeed. My wife, Lisa, cannot rebound from a tragic loss. My promise of a DaVinci portrait could help the healing. In fact," Giocondo takes a long pause, "It may be the only way she will rise from the abyss."

DaVinci is annoyed. "Enough theatrics, Mr. Giocondo. What do you really want from me?"

"Your original portrait of Lisa for my home. Our home. And one hand can wash the other.'"

DaVinci nods and gestures for Giocondo to pay very close attention. At lightening speed, DaVinci flips through all the pages of the small codex to animate the drawings.

Giocondo is impressed and intrigued.

DaVinci explains, "This is how I would paint The Battle of Anghiari on the walls. With obsessive warriors willing to die for a victorious Republic. Mano-a-mano, medieval sword-to-sword across The Hall of The Five Hundred. The edifice on the Palazzo Vecchio that Savonarola managed to finish building —just before he was hanged, then burned at the stake. Talk about overkill."

Giocondo is surprised. "How did you know I am on the selection committee? That I could influence who would be chosen to paint those massive frescos."

"You told the genius me to figure it out," DaVinci responds, nonchalantly.

"Many fine artists are vying for that commission," Giocondo remarks. "Including Miche…"

DaVinci interrupts. "Please do not say his name in my presence."

Giocondo manages to name the name without naming. "Then I will call him Mr. Pietà."

DaVinci replies, "That filthy boy will neither paint the battle scenes in question. Nor paint a portrait of your wife." He continues with conviction. "I will do both."

FIVE YEARS EARLIER, DAVINCI IS SITTING BY THE ARNO River where all is quiet and serene. His hair is less grey, his beard is much shorter. Dressed in his trademark pastel tunic and cap, he sketches in a small codex, watching the little egrets fly over the river in search of tadpole and fish.

A rowdy group approaches. They are all slim, athletic and handsome young men who have never met a bar of soap or had a bath in the recent past.

The young men follow an equally young charismatic leader who points at DaVinci and gets in his face. This is Michelangelo, slovenly as ever.

Michelangelo starts taunting DaVinci. "I knew you'd be here, old man. Watching the birds dive bomb for food. Maybe to inspire a flying machine? That's a joke. You're a joke."

DaVinci ignores Michelangelo and keeps on sketching.

"The Last Supper is history, DaVinci," taunts Michelangelo. "The last true mediocrity in your over-hyped career. On the contrary, my brilliant future is guaranteed. With the pope's generous offer to paint a ceiling while lying flat on my back. You? You couldn't even climb the scaffold."

DaVinci looks up at a little egret circling overhead.

"My current project?" Michelangelo boasts, "A biblical hero seventeen feet high. Carved from the marble slab you nearly sent to the scrap heap with a sad attempt at sculpting Hercules."

Michelangelo laughs and the great unwashed follow suit. A little egret flies down and craps all over Michelangelo's head and shoulders. DaVinci smiles and keeps right on sketching.

Defiant, Michelangelo says, "You think a little bird crap bothers me, Leonardo retardo?

I say...the more shit...the more authentic the artist...the more authentic the art."

Michelangelo gives DaVinci the Italian *gesto dell'ombrello* —that ever-popular, much-used obscene gesture. Then, at the top of his lungs, he yells "Ciao, loser!"

Hooting and hollering, they all leave DaVinci sitting there. Alone, he's content to sketch nature's aerialists swoop and dive on the picturesque banks of the great Tuscan river.

RETURN TO GIOCONDO AS HE WALKS TOWARD HIS NEW, Medici-adjacent mansion. He carries a huge bouquet of light purple, dark purple and blue-veined white iris. He opens the front door and enters a heavily fabric-centric interior that's accented with winged sculptures, a fireplace with carved angels and serious Giocondo family portraits intermingled with paintings of heavenly cherubim.

Giocondo continues walking through the main floor, travelling through the large dining room and finally into the larger kitchen. Here, Lisa is expertly pruning many different species of plants that she has proudly displayed on the expansive windowsill.

"These are for you, my love," Giocondo gushes.

Lisa opens one of many cabinets, finds a beautiful Murano glass vase and fills it with water.

"Feeling guilty Francesco?" she asks, taking the flowers stem by stem and arranging them artfully in the vase. "I can't remember your bringing me flowers. Because you never have."

Giocondo feigns hurt feelings. "Harsh. Sooo harsh. And a lie. You only remember everything I buy for you and do for you when it's convenient. I deserve an apology, Lisa. Say you're sorry."

"I remember our other life at our other home," she says.

"The flowers," Giocodo says, "are to thank you for not bringing more winged things into every room here. Including all the empty rooms upstairs waiting for children to bless them."

Lisa shakes her head and continues the floral arrangement.

"Of course," he continues, "we have to behave like a normal married couple to create those blessed children. Are you hearing what I'm saying to you, Lisa?"

Giocondo takes a stem out of the vase, picks the petals off, and lets them fall to the floor.

"I'm sure you'll be procreating with another woman," Lisa says. "I am sorry, Francesco.

I meant other women." Vase in hand, she walks to the dining room and puts it on the table.

Giocondo follows her.

Calmly, he says, "I met with DaVinci again, Lisa. He is eager to paint your portrait."

She refuses to even glance at her husband. "I said no."

"As part of the transaction, I asked him, I begged him - to include some sketches of our dear baby Francesca." Near crocodile tears, his voice is quivering. "Her curly hair, her eyes, her tiny mouth." Giocondo pauses perfectly, "The way she still lives in your mind's eye."

Lisa leans over to smell the flowers on the table.

"He said yes."

She stands up straight. She looks at her husband. Acquiescing, she slowly nods her head.

DAYS LATER, DAVINCI IS OUTSIDE IN THE SMALL courtyard where it is very hot, sunny and still.

Dressed in lighter fabrics, he sits on one of the three chairs that surround the table where there are large glasses, folded linen napkins and three glass carafes filled with colorful juices.

Dressed in opulent layers that defy the temperature, a smiling Giocondo enters. Lisa enters steps behind him, carrying a small basket. Sweating, her hair done up and her head way down, she is dressed like a Renaissance courtesan about to be ravished on some ballroom balcony.

DaVinci smiles and stands to greet them.

"Maestro. Mr. DaVinci," says Giocondo, "May I proudly introduce my wife. LaGioconda. The Lady Lisa. The Mona Lisa."

Lisa, her head still bowed, responds. Quietly, she says, "Lisa."

DaVinci holds out his hand for her to shake. Quietly, he says "Leo."

Gicondo mouths the name 'Leo' and nearly has a coronary.

Lisa reluctantly shakes DaVinci's hand. He keeps holding

her hand, leads her toward the table and pulls out a chair for her. Nearly passing out, Lisa removes some of her heavy brocade outerwear. Then her shoes. DaVinci takes off his shoes. With a sigh of relief, Lisa sits down with the basket on her lap, then covers her mouth with her hand. Shoes still on, an unhappy Giocondo takes a seat. DaVinci sits back in his original chair. "Please, drink." DaVinci points to the three different carafes. "Fresh orange. Peach. Pomegranate. Lisa?"

Lisa, her eyes wide with anticipation, can only point. DaVinci pours her a glass of peach juice. "Peach. Good choice." DaVinci pours a glass of pomegranate juice for Giocondo and a glass of orange juice for himself. DaVinci raises his glass, Giocondo raises his, Lisa raises hers. "To art," DaVinci toasts. The men sip. Lisa downs her juice in one gulp.

Lisa pushes up her long sleeves, then takes a napkin, unfolds it and wipes her face.

"Give him the basket, Lisa," Giocondo instructs her. Lisa hands the basket to DaVinci.

DaVinci takes the basket, looks inside and responds with sincere delight. "Sugar cakes!

I haven't had sugar cakes since I was an unhappy little boy in Vinci." He immediately eats two.

"I can never find these in the market. Grazie, Lisa." He chews with remembrance.

"She didn't find them, Sir. She made them." Giocondo states. "She also made the basket."

A shocked DaVinci says, "No? The basket? How?"

Lisa, with quiet humility, says, "Soaking small branches of willow and reed. Then weaving."

Giocondo interrupts and points to the basket's interior. "Did you see the silk lining?"

DaVinci ignores Giocondo and says, "Now, Lisa, I must

to do something special for you. First, help yourself to more juice."

DaVinci stands as Lisa fills her glass with peach juice. He takes off his hat, ready to work. Step by step, he will narrate the spectacle literally about to unfold.

DaVinci explains, "I will begin to unfurl the sailcloth that I have attached to spokes of rope. He walks toward the first set-up, constructed between one tree and another.

"Observe," he continues, "how I employ a combination of wheels and pulleys." DaVinci manipulates the equipment and shades rise. "I was inspired by the verarium...ver-ar-i-um. The most significant system of awnings invented in the ancient world."

Giocondo watches the progress with ennui. Lisa drinks her juice, awestruck.

DaVinci goes to the second set- up, constructed between a bench and the statue of Mary. "The verarium was the massive complex of shade structures deployed above the many different seating areas of the Roman Colosseum."

DaVinci is having trouble turning the larger pulley by the statue of Mary.

Although tired, DaVinci continues his descriptive narrative. "They made sure the awnings could be extended or retracted according to the position of the sun." He pauses to catch his breath. "So the Christians and the lions could stay cool all day long."

"Mr. Giocondo," frustrated, DaVinci asks, "Could you help me turn this?"

Giocondo, staying seated, responds, "I have no mechanical ability, Sir. So"

Lisa cuts her husband off and says, "I do." She jumps up, races over to the problem pulley and turns it like she's captain of the SS Gherardini, her maiden name. With her hair coming undone and her skirt in a bunch, Lisa is one proud farm girl.

Now, all shades rise above the table and chairs, flapping like bird wings against the blue sky.

"Brava, Mona Lisa! Bravissimo!" DaVinci exclaims.

For a brief but poignant moment, Lisa puts her hands on Mary's hands. Then, she and DaVinci walk together back to the table, sit down and enjoy the shade. DaVinci drinks the orange juice right out of the carafe. Lisa does the same with the peach juice. Giocondo is disgusted.

Lisa puts her hand over her mouth as Giocondo begins to pontificate. "I assume, Mr. DaVinci, the material used here," Giocondo points up, "is heavy canvas made from linen woven in Venice."

"Yes," Mr. Giocondo." DaVinci replies. "The Venetians always supply me with the best canvas available. Whatever I happen to be working on at any given moment."

Suddenly, two little skylarks fly into the garden and land in the birdbath. They splish and splash for a few minutes to cool off. "Skylarks," Lisa says softly. Giocondo, knowing his wife well, tries to stop her as she stands up.

With graceful stealth, Lisa tiptoes toward the birdbath. When she gets close enough, she stands there, statue-like and barely breathing. Slowly, she extends one arm out parallel to her body. One skylark keeps on splashing. The other skylark stops and acknowledges Lisa.

That skylark takes a direct flight out of the birdbath and lands on Lisa's outstretched arm. To get a better look, the skylark hops closer to Lisa's face. And chirps. They stare at each other. Finally, the skylark decides to take off and land back with his friend in the birdbath.

DaVinci looks at Giocondo. "I believe your wife will be

able to sit, unmoving, for hours at a time." Giocondo nods his head with an I-told-you-so look on his face.

"Time for us to have a change of scene." DaVinci teases, "I regret to inform you, Lisa, the birds must stay outside in their natural habit. Now. Please follow me."

DaVinci starts to lead them toward the bookcase door, but he suddenly stops and turns around. "I almost forgot Lisa's marvelous basket of sugar cakes. The monks have an ungodly sweet tooth." DaVinci returns to the table, takes the basket and resumes leading Mr. and Mrs. Giocondo inside.

THEY ARE NOW IN DAVINCI'S STUDIO. LISA SITS ON THE same chair several feet from DaVinci, just as her husband did weeks ago. Her head is bowed, her hand covers her mouth. DaVinci, sitting on the wooden stool with a cushion top, has yet another large codex that is open on his lap.

"Lisa, my dear." says DaVinci,"For your comfort, why not change into one of the long white smocks hanging on the rack." DaVinci points to the location. "Your choice."

"I will do the choosing," Giocondo says. He and Lisa walk toward the rack. Giocondo inspects smock after smock and makes the choice. "Nice embroidery," he says with authority.

DaVinci explains, "Behind the rack is a dressing room, Lisa. Where you can also freshen up."

Giocondo hands Lisa the smock and nods his head. As she leaves to find the dressing room, he automatically sits down in the chair facing DaVinci.

DaVinci starts sketching in the codex. "I am very impressed with your wife," he says.

"More impressed than with me, I imagine." Giocondo answers.

"Not necessarily," DaVinci comments. "Although the two of you do seem a bit misaligned."

"Maestro," Giocondo says with emphasis. "That is an understatement."

DaVinci, still sketching, says "There is definitely something amiss." Giocondo nods his head.

"I noticed that Lisa keeps covering her mouth." DaVinci continues. "Never a grin. Not even a hint of one. There could be a muscle disorder affecting the depressor anguli oris, therisorius, the zygomaticus major, the zygomaticus minor and levator labii superioris. Or, perhaps, the orbicularis oris that pulls all those muscles upward could be compromised.

"Or perhaps," Giocondo responds sarcastically, "My wife is feeling very sorry for herself."

Always sketching, DaVinci continues, "About what, Mr. Giocondo?"

Giocondo shrugs his shoulders. "Feel free to ask."

"I will. But I would like to ask you about the Ospedale degli Innocenti: the foundling hospital directly across from the basilica."

"What about it," Giocondo answers with disinterest.

"I have spent many long days and nights there, Mr. Giocondo." DaVinci explains,

"You don't look like a baby nurse to me."

DaVinci laughs. "Anatomy and skilled surgery are mandatory in a doctor's curriculum.

They have been generous enough to let me learn with the medical students. Side-by-side."

Giocodo sticks a forefinger in his mouth and makes a

gagging noise.

"How the body works is a mechanical marvel, Mr. Giocondo,"says DaVinci. "That knowledge makes my work more accurate. Whether I'm painting a portrait or designing an underwater diving suit. But I mention the foundlings for a reason. In the basement, there are portraits of charitable patrons who have donated great sums to the hospital's expansion. The most imposing portrait is that of a man who looks exactly like you." DaVinci is still sketching away.

Giocondo laughs, then gets serious. "I spend money and make money to spend more. I do not give money away. Ever. When Lisa's father was down on his luck, I still cut the dowry he expected by fifty percent. Because I could. And to answer your question. It was The Arte della Seta, the silk guild, who ponied up for the Ospedale degli Innocenti. With every coin of that exorbitant funding managed by my oh-so-benevolent older brother."

Wearing the crisp white smock, skin glowing and hair flowing, Lisa returns - refreshed. Giocondo stands and moves to the side of the chair. Lisa walks behind DaVinci and sees the sketch he's just finished drawing.

"Francesco. Leo's drawing looks just like your older brother," Lisa comments. Giocondo walks over, takes a glance and shrugs. Lisa sits down to face DaVinci, who turns to a blank page in his codex. She immediately covers her mouth with her hand.

Giocondo commands, "Take your hand away from your mouth, Lisa. I mean it. Right now,"

Lisa takes her hand away from her mouth. Then, takes her other hand and covers her mouth.

DaVinci puts the codex down and walks to Lisa. He squats in front of her and pats her knee.

"If we work together as portrait artist and portrait subject, I must be honest with you. And you must be honest with me. That will be the rule of this adventure. Nod if you concur."

Lisa nods.

"Honestly, Lisa," DaVinci asks kindly, "Why do you cover your mouth."

Lisa pauses. Then, in a whisper, she responds, "Teeth."

DaVinci responds, "Teeth?"

Giocondo responds, "Yes. She's trying to hide her horrible, terrible teeth. Nearly gray from all that torrone she's devoured since I brought her to the city. Where sugar is plentiful for the rich. The devil hides in those long rectangles of sticky, honey confection full of almonds."

DaVinci explains, "The Venetians toast the almonds much longer, so their mandorlato is a richer-tasting torrrone. My opinion? Any nougat from the south of France is far, far superior."

Giocondo, frustrated, says, "Et tu, Maestro?"

Lisa puts her clenched hands in her lap and starts to relax just a bit.

DaVinci stands up, goes back to his cushion-topped stool, picks up his codex and opens it yet again. "Lisa. Very slowly, please turn your head to one side. Then to the other side."

Lisa follows his instructions perfectly.

DaVinci continues. "Excellent, my dear Mona Lisa. Now. Turn your whole body to one side. Then to the other side. Please. Take your time."

Again, Lisa follows his instructions.

Giocondo, not one to stay neutral, intervenes. He grabs his wife and pushes her into a more exaggerated position. "He said your whole body. Not just your shoulders."

DaVinci stands up, walks to Lisa, and gently adjusts her shoulders to a more natural position.

Giocondo pushes her shoulders to his preferred, more exaggerated position. They repeat the action.

Finally, DaVinci returns to his wooden stool and starts to sketch. Lisa is so upset with the repositioning, she turns completely around - so her back is to DaVinci. Giocondo is furious.

DaVinci puts the codex down. "It's been a long day," he says. "Why not revisit the courtyard?" He stands up. "I'm sure the monks have delivered a lovely offering of Amarone wine for us to drink out there. They've been making it themselves since the thirteenth century."

Giocondo, more than ready to leave, comments. "It has to be better than the pomegranate juice."

He walks toward the door.

As Lisa starts to follow her husband, DaVinci whispers in her ear, "The ancient Egyptians invented a formula to whiten their discolored teeth. I will make it for you, Lisa."

MR. AND MRS. GIOCONDO ARE SITTING INSIDE A MOVING carriage. He drinks from a bottle of Amarone. Pulled by one horse on an unpaved road, the short journey from the basilica to their mansion is rocky. Literally and figuratively.

They ride in silence for quite a while.

Giocondo finally speaks up. "Those monks really know how to make a good Amarone."

Not only does Lisa not respond, she moves even further away from her husband.

"Ah, your old standby. The silent treatment," he says. "Well, I have plenty to say, Lisa. I will start by telling you a story. Once upon a time, I knew a woman who had no teeth. No uppers. No lowers. Nada. She was a lovely woman. A natural blonde. Quite accomplished. And very, very popular with men. The reason she was very, very popular with men is because she had no teeth.

Do you understand her popularity, Lisa?"

"You are disgusting," Lisa says under her breath.

"I'd rather be disgusting than someone making a fool of herself in front of the world's greatest artist, inventor and thinker. I wouldn't be surprised at all, Mrs. Giocondo, if he no longer wants to paint your portrait." Giocondo takes a big Amarone gulp.

Lisa looks at her husband, confused.

Giocondo continues. "Next month, when I return from my trip to Genoa, DaVinci is planning to visit one of our larger silk workshops. Which is when, with all likelihood, he will bow out."

The carriage finally stops in front of their new mansion.

Giocondo sits in the carriage. Unmoving and seething, he chugs the wine.

Lisa, wordlessly, opens the door and quickly exits the carriage. She lovingly strokes the horse's face and whispers to the animal, "Don't worry, Cavallo. Leo is not that kind of man."

THE PALAZZO VECCHIO IS THE TOWN HALL OF FLORENCE. Outside, many people enter and exit the building on city business. The Hall of The Five Hundred is on the first floor.

Michelangelo, unkempt and covered with marble dust, stands looking up at the magnificent architecture. DaVinci stands looking up at the large clock on the building. They are quite a distance apart. They sense each other's presence, but neither one is willing to acknowledge the other. People seem too preoccupied to recognize either man.

The two artists are about to have a conversation. Voices and hackles will be raised. The more they speak at one another, the louder Michelangelo's voice will become. Finally, his vociferous accusations get so loud, bystanders will stop to witness his juvenile behavior.

Michelangelo points to the first floor of the building. "Hall of The Five Hundred. Mine."

DaVinci shakes his head and smiles. "Hall of The Five Hundred. Mine."

Michelangelo: "Mine."

DaVinci: "The Battle of Anghiari. Mine."

Michelangelo: "The Battle of Cascina. Mine."

DaVinci: "East wall."

Michelangelo: "West wall. The west wall is the best wall."

DaVinci: "Sun rises in the east, Mr. Buonarroti. This is my commission to win, not lose."

Michelangelo: "Then why am I so comfortable calling you Leo the Loser, Leo the Loser."

The two men turn and start walking away from one another. As if choreographed, they simultaneously turn around and walk back even closer. Now, Michelangelo gets even louder.

DaVinci: "I have a patron."

Michelangelo: "I have a patron."

DaVinci: "A powerful patron"

Michelangelo: "Mine is the patron of patrons. Even if your

so-called patron could secure a commission, you would never finish. You bail. You fail. Over and over again."

DaVinci: "Art is never finished, only abandoned."

Michelangelo: "That is an expected excuse from a bona fide quitter."

DaVinci: "And you? You will never even start," he says, definitively.

Michelangelo: "Who says."

DaVinci, frustrated and defiant, finally raises his voice. "So says Leonardo DaVinci!"

The bystanders applaud. Michelangelo, stomping his feet like a toddler, delivers a very loud and unbecoming raspberry directed toward DaVinci. The bystanders boo. Michelangelo leaves in a huff. DaVinci exists quietly. Everyone is buzzing about Florence's best and brightest.

A WEEK OR SO LATER, LISA IS VISITING THE OSPEDALE degli Innocenti. She visits the hospital often and the nuns there know her well.

One of the ornate trunks from the former Giocondo residence is in a playroom. Children's drawings hang on the walls and handmade birds dangle from the ceiling on colorful ribbons. Long tables are flanked by long benches. There are oversized baskets filled with breads of all shapes and sizes. Lisa is about to open the trunk, and the two nuns in the room can barely contain themselves.

Nun #1 says, "You are one of our favorite visitors, La Gioconda."

Nun #2 says, "And not because you bake bread and biscuits

for all our poor little children."

"It is my joy to bring them whatever I can," explains Lisa. "But only what I can afford, considering my meager allowance."

"I will give your husband a piece of my mind," says Nun #2. "If he ever shows up here."

Lisa unlocks the trunk. "Ready, Sisters?" she asks. The nuns nod with anticipation. Inside the trunk is everything that used to occupy a very happy place in the very pink Giocondo nursery.

One by one, Lisa takes out baby clothing and holds every tiny item close to her chest. The nuns "ooo" and "ahh" with great delight. Lisa takes out the menagerie of stuffed sheep and little lambs, pets them and gently places them on the floor.

"You are brave, Lisa," says Nun #1. "Our Lady of Sorrows recognizes you from heaven."

"Mother Mary is always here to give you solace," says Nun #2.

"Because she lost a child, as well," sadly says Nun #1.

When most of the contents have been removed from the trunk, Lisa stares at the emptiness inside. She notices two items remaining.

She picks up the music box, turns it on and hands it to one of the nuns.

She picks up one of her homemade birds still attached to its colorful ribbon.

"Crib, rocking chair and other nursery furniture will be delivered tomorrow," Lisa whispers.

"Bless you, Mona Lisa," says an emotional Nun #1.

"And Francesca," echoes Nun #2.

Lisa leaves, still cradling the one delicate bird she could not bear to leave behind.

ONE MONTH LATER, GIOCONDO HAS RETURNED FROM Genoa. The foyer of his workshop is a study in opulence. Silk on the walls. Silk pillows piled high. Lifelike mannequins lavishly costumed in silk.

Adjacent is a luxurious office suite. Giocondo stands with his back to the door, studying some ledger books open on an impressive desk. As close as possible, a pair of red-headed, green-eyed twins in skin-tight silk stand next to Giocondo. Amili has her right hand on his left butt cheek. Her sister, Nomili, has her left hand on his right butt cheek. Ah, the birth of Venus…times two.

DaVinci has arrived and is waiting outside Giocondo's office. The threesome inside has not escaped DaVinci's attention. He shakes his head and loudly clears his throat. Nomili turns around, sees DaVinci and, with confidence, keeps her hand on Giocondo's butt.

"Oh, Francesco," she informs him. "Your honored guest has arrived."

Giocondo walks toward DaVinci and gestures for him to enter the office. "Welcome, Sir," says an obsequious Giocondo. "We have been counting the days."

"We?" asks DaVinci.

"Yes, the twins are bursting to meet you," explains Giocondo.

"Bursting, ladies?" DaVinci teases.

Amili walks to DaVinci and curtsies. "My name is Amili. Ami."

Nomili walks to DaVinci and curtsies. "My name is Nomili. Nomi."

Giocondo says, "Ami and Nomi are my personal assistants. I could not manage all my businesses without them. Well, I could. But it certainly would not be as stimulating."

Ami and Nomi laugh and toss their red hair simultaneously.

"I should introduce both of you to my friend, Sandro Botticelli," suggests DaVinci.

Ami and Nomi laugh and toss their red hair simultaneously —in the opposite direction.

Giocondo, eager to change focus, says, "The twins will make sure lunch is ready after our tour of the workshop. Run along, my double trouble. Svelto! Immediamente!"

The twins sashay out.

"How do you tell them apart, Mr. Giocondo?" DaVinci asks politely.

Giocondo nonchalantely answers, "What's the difference. They're both the same in the dark. Enough about the twins. It's time for you to visit the most productive silk workshop in the world. Exporting internationally to France, Flanders, England, Spain, Constantinople and Alexandria." Giocondo continues his exposition, "Now, Maestro, come with me. And meet my little silkworms, which is what I call the artisans who practically invented the process."

AROUND THE YEAR 2696 BC, LEGEND HAS IT THAT THE process for making silk cloth was first invented by Leizu, the wife of the Yellow Emperor. Obviously legend, not known for being politically correct, had no reservations about calling the Chinese emperor yellow.

The idea for silk first came to Empress Yellow while she was having tea in the imperial gardens. A cocoon fell into her tea and unraveled. She noticed that the cocoon was actually made from a long thread that felt both strong and soft. It may have been the tea that was both strong and soft (and hallucinogenic) but we will never know.

Empress Yellow then discovered how to combine the silk fibers into a viable thread.

She also invented the silk loom that combined the threads into a soft cloth.

Subsequently, Empress Yellow ordered her husband to plant a forest of mulberry trees for the silkworms to feed on... and thrive in...like no other silkworms had ever thrived and fed before.

So enamored by worm proliferation and cloth sophistication, Empress Yellow resolved to teach all of China how to make silk. But her misfortune cookie didn't factor in the fibers unevenly bumping, lumping and clumping the filament thread. Which slowed any warp speed to a crawl.

THE EXPANSIVE LOOM ROOM IN GIOCONDO'S WORKSHOP is spotlessly-clean and well-lit...with endless spools of thread manipulated by weavers of all shapes, sexes, ages and ethnicities. All creating silk fabric, lace and ribbons in bold colors favored by the over-the-top House of Medici.

A feast for the eyes, yet eerily quiet. Except for a constant hum of a soothing symphony, orchestrated by each weaver at each hand loom working to his or her own unique rhythm.

One man in particular seems to be the symphony

conductor. Older, stooped and slow, he oversees Giocondo's little silkworms with the confidence that comes with a lifetime of experience.

Giocondo, entering with DaVinci, behaves like he's a combination of babbling tour guide and circus ring master. The artisans don't stop their work, not even for him.

"They don't stop, even for me," Giocondo pontificates. "Because it takes at least eight hours to produce two yards of silk. Favored by kings, queens, maharajas, and of course, Lorenzo."

The older man walks painfully toward Giocondo and DaVinci.

Giocondo remarks, "This is the man, along with myself, most responsible for the success of the globally famous Florentine silk guild. May I introduce"

DaVinci interrupts and says, "DeLuca."

Deluca, squinting, says, "DaVinci."

Giocondo, slaps his forehead in disbelief. DaVinci and Deluca, thrilled, kiss each other on both cheeks, twice.

"You have a beard." says DeLuca, amazed. "It has turned gray."

"It's been thirty years," says DaVinci, equally amazed.

"I am so old I should be dead by now," DeLuca says, matter-of-factly.

Giocondo, confused, points at the two men, asks, "Why... where...when?"

DeLuca sees a broom leaning against the wall. He picks it up and says, "One day, a serious young man wanders into the loom room," says DeLuca. He hands the broom to DaVinci. "I give him a broom and tell him to start sweeping."

DaVinci says, "So I start sweeping. But I tell DeLuca I don't need a job. I'm an artist and an inventor curious about how things work."

DeLuca taps his temple with his forefinger, indicating crazy. "Pazzo Meccanico," he says.

DaVinci tries handing the broom to Giocondo who won't even touch it. DeLuca takes the broom and leans it back against the wall. He walks toward one of the loom workers. DaVinci and Giocondo follow DeLuca.

"Weeks go by," Deluca continues, pointing at DaVinci, "and Pazzo Meccanico is here every single day. Then one day, the weavers are working twice as fast as they did the day before."

Giocondo says proudly, "My little silkworms. Ramping up production."

DeLuca stands behind one of the weavers and gestures for DaVinci to stand with him. Then, DeLuca taps the weaver three times on her shoulder. What follows is a changing of the weavers. Without losing any rhythm, she and DaVinci switch places. She stands up, DaVinci sits down at the loom, and he continues the weaving process seamlessly.

Giocondo, exasperated, says, "What. You're a maestro of silk-weaving, too?"

DeLuca gestures toward some specific moving parts of the loom that DaVinci continues to operate. DeLuca announces, "Young DaVinci invented The Zetto."

Giocondo repeats, "The Zetto?"

All the weavers in the room, proudly repeat, "The Zetto!"

DeLuca continues, "He re-engineered thread-spinning by using a pole to stop any bumps, lumps or clumps. Now, every fiber wraps evenly on the spool, so the filament is more uniform." DeLuca stretches a long, imaginary piece with ease. "Bellisimo."

The twins barge into the loom room. They are very upset.

"The wine, Francesco!" Ami explains. "May not be the

47

right temperature!" Nomi exclaims.

Giodondo says, calmly, "Excuse me, this emergency must be averted."

Giocondo exits with the twins. DeLuca taps DaVinci three times on the shoulder. He stands up

and, without missing a beat, the original weaver takes her rightful place back at the loom.

DaVinci and DeLuca find a place to sit among a dazzling pile of sumptuous silk.

"You are painting the portrait of LaGioconda," DeLuca says to DaVinci.

Davinci shrugs his shoulders and smiles.

DeLuca continues, "I may be going deaf, but I hear everything."

DaVinci kindly says, "She intrigues me. There's a purity. Not spiritual. Natural."

DeLuca leans forward and says, "Francesco does not deserve her. Lisa has a heart as big as a mulberry forest. Unlike other members of the Giocondo family, Francesco is a heartless man.

The day their baby died, he was in his palatial office. I was here. I saw him. With the twins."

Quietly, DaVinci says, "People grieve in different ways, my long-lost friend."

"You have to feel grief to grieve", DeLuca responds. "Don't tell the boss, but I collect all the scraps of silk and lace and ribbons for her. I have for some time. Then I have the fabric boxed and delivered to the Ospedale degli Innocenti for Lisa to pick up."

DaVinci asks, "Why?"

DeLuca says, "She is an accomplished craftsman in her

own right."

The twins barge in yet again. "Luncheon is served, Maestro," says Ami. "Please come with us," says Nomi.

DaVinci hugs DeLuca. "We will see each other soon, DeLuca," DaVinci promises.

"Say a prayer, DaVinci," DeLuca responds.

Ami takes one of DaVinci's hands, Nomi takes the other. They leave the loom room.

DaVinci and the twins enter a room that could only belong in Caesar's palace. The one that existed in Rome 46 BC, and the one still dishing it out in Vegas. Talk about a Bacchanal buffet,

Giocondo obviously went above and beyond to make sure Lisa's portrait gets painted.

Covered with linen, flowers and candles, two long buffet tables are next to each other at right angles. In the middle of the two tables is a smaller table with two facing throne-like chairs.

"I hope you're hungry," Giocondo says to DaVinci.

DaVinci is hesitant to answer. "More thirsty than hungry, Mr. Giocondo."

The twins stand at the ready to serve. Giocondo gestures for DaVinci to join him and peruse the embarrassment of epicurean riches. "Don't worry, Maestro. I sent one of my favorite cooks to meet your cook at the basilica," says Giocondo.

"How did you know I had a cook?"

"One of the monks let the secret slip." Giocondo jokes. "So did the cook. Let me show you."

Giocondo takes DaVinci's arm and slowly leads him down the extravagant, yet meatless table. "You are the first vegetarian I have ever dined with. Except for Lisa. Yet, somehow, she can never resist a trout with almonds."

DaVinci explains, "A day will come when men will look upon an animal's murder the same way they look today upon a man's murder. So I very much appreciate your thoughtful menu to satisfy my often difficult demands."

Giocondo tries to lighten up the conversation. He jokes, "I guess you won't be sharing the goat kid's pie and roasted pheasant with me. What about cheeses?"

DaVinci says, "Jesus is always welcome at a feast. He would certainly enjoy the magnificent mix of color and texture of all these salads."

Ami puts some salad on a plate along with a big hunk of white bread and butter. She brings it to the small table.

"The rice balls, golden leeks with onion, the artichokes, marvelous," continues DaVinci.

Nomi puts rice balls, leeks and artichokes on another plate and brings it to the small table.

"Ah, chick pea soup." DaVinci says. "Try it, Mr Giocondo. It is my own special recipe."

Ami ladles the soup into one bowl, then into another. She takes both bowls and brings them to the small table. Ami and Nomi both go to the meat-laden table, fill plates with tasty bites and breads for Giocondo and bring them to the small table. The men sit across from each other.

Giocondo asks DaVinci, "Juice? Wine? Ale? Tea? I prefer we make a toast with wine."

DaVinci says, "Trebbiano. Cold as an Alpine winter."

"I adjusted the temperature myself," boasts Giocondo.

"Yes he did," Ami and Nomi respond in stereo. Then, the twins exit in a hurry.

"Try the soup while it's hot," suggests DaVinci. He digs in with a silver spoon.

Giocondo tries a spoonful. Then another. Then another. He nods with approval.

The twins return. Ami carries two wine bottles. Nomi carries two fancy glasses. Ami puts the bottles down on the table. Nomi puts glasses on the table, then carefully fills both of them with a very heavy pour. Giocondo nods to the twins. They exit.

Giocondo stands and dramatically raises his glass. DaVinci stands and raises his glass.

"To the unsung, understated chick pea," toasts Giocondo. They clink glasses, drink, sit back down, then earnestly begin to sample the abundant repast. The two men enjoy the dining experience in silence for a time.

"You have been travelling, Mr. Giocondo?" DaVinci asks, wiping his mouth with a napkin.

"To Genoa. I spent nearly a month there," Giocondo answers.

"I hope you and Lisa had many opportunities to taste the varieties of pesto they serve. Pesto was, in fact, created in Genoa. My cook, in fact, was created in Genoa, as well. And only uses Genovese basil. So I am blessed with the star of vegetarian cuisine on many days and nights." Giocondo chews his food slowly before he responds.

"No," confesses Giocondo. "My wife did not accompany me to Genoa. My financial associates and I were there solely on banking business. She would have been bored to tears."

"You are dissatisfied with the Medici Bank in Florence?" asks DaVinci, surprised.

Giocondo says, "Both of my guilds are well represented there. But at the Bank of St. George in Genoa, a board of directors owns the company. I am one of the pre-eminent directors. And yes, I did take time to enjoy a plate of pesto. And remember one of my acquaintances, Mr. Columbus."

DaVinci says, "You met with Christopher Columbus? Impressive. I never had the pleasure."

Giocondo teases him, "I thought you knew everyone."

DaVinci laughs, "He and I are like ships passing in the night."

"I met with the family of Christopher Columbus," Giocondo continues. "Paying my respects to Domenico, his father who recently passed. He was a master weaver of the blue wool cloth created in Genoa. Very popular for durability with sailors in and out of the seaport."

"You must be happy to be home," says DaVinci. "A month away can often feel infinite."

"I'm sorry I wasn't here for the last committee meeting about The Hall of The Five Hundred.

Is the jury still out?" Giocondo asks.

"Michelangelo just received a commission for the West wall," states DaVinci.

"My apologies, Maestro," says Giocondo, sincerely. "Who gave him patronage?"

"Machiavelli. Who was also my patron for the East wall," reveals DaVinci. "Not a surprise. Nicolo loves every aspect of war. He likes to say 'Never do an enemy a small injury'. Our paintings? The bloodier the better. To the death. I am a pacifist, may God forgive me. "

"Michelangelo Buonarrati and Leonard DaVinci painting at

the same time in the same place?" asks Giocondo, stunned.

"I have no problem with that. As long as he stays downwind," jokes DaVinci.

Nomi and Ami return to refill the wine glasses and quickly clear plates from the small table. DaVinci says to Giocondo, "I hope your cook and mine have arranged to donate the leftover food to the struggling poor. Too much in the midst of too little is a sin."

Giocondo says, "Of course, Maestro. It would never go to waste." Then, with some sarcasm, Giocondo adds, "My wife, Saint Lisa, will be eager to assure you of that." Then, with some pride, he adds, "And our guild workers can take any of the food remaining home for their families to enjoy. That is how we roll. " Giocondo picks up a roll to illustrate his incredible wit.

"While I was in Genoa," Giocondo continues, "the Columbus family gifted me with a treasure trove from Christopher's travels all around the world. I am thrilled to share two of the more exotic treasures with you now."

Ami enters with a silver pot. Nomi follows with a tray of cups and saucers, sugar and cream. Steaming hot coffee is poured. The twins leave. Both men smell the aroma and are captivated.

"The beverage is called coffee," Giocondo explains. "African coffee beans picked by hand and roasted in small batches." The men take a sip. "My cook pounded the beans into a fine grind, put the contents into cheesecloth, then poured boiling water over and let it drip. Opinion?"

"Interesting. But slightly bitter for my taste," DaVinci says.

"Add some sugar and cream. Like this," says Giocondo, adds some cream and sugar to his cup. DaVinci adds cream and a lot of sugar, swirls the coffee with his spoon and sips again.

"Yes, I could alternate this coffee with my favorite juices," declares DaVinci.

Giocondo adds, "The beverage is rumored to produce energetic results. Which I am sure you will appreciate during the daunting battle of fresco painting on the East wall."

"Machiavelli also offered to finance some of my inventions," says DaVinci. "Tank, catapult, cross bow, helicopter, parachute, triple-barrel canon, et cetera. Bring on the coffee!"

Giocondo's face drops. The twins return with two pineapples, a wooden tray, a large carving knife, and extra folded linen napkins.

"These are pineapple fruits, Maestro," announces Ami.

Giocondo says, "Not a pine. Not an apple."

DaVinci comments, "The exterior appears to be a honeycomb-like array of hexagons. Similar to the Paleodictyon, an enigmatic trace fossil.

Giocondo tries to one-up DaVinci. "I learned that pineapples actually grow on a plant close to the ground. In a place called The Bahamas. Each pineapple plant bears only one pineapple."

"Nature delights in such variety that one plant is never exactly like another," DaVinci says.

Giocondo has a smarmy response. "The same goes for women."

The twins giggle. Ami puts one pineapple on the tray, picks up the knife and expertly separates the peel from the flesh. She hands the knife to Nomi who cuts the flesh in half, removes the core and cuts the fruit into a masterful combination of slices and pieces. Giocondo picks up a slice with his fingers and devours it. DaVinci follows his lead.

"You are spoiling me, Mr. Giocondo," admits DaVinci. "I

appreciate the experience."

"Please," Giocondo replies. "Take the other pineapple with you as a gift."

DaVinci eats more and more pineapple and chews it with gusto. Then says, "I will gladly take the pineapple with me. So I can share its bright yellow delight with Lisa when she returns to sit for me. At your convenience. Later this week."

Giocondo, eagerly wiping his hands with a linen napkin and obviously relieved, says, "With the weight of all the new commissions, I thought you would abandon her portrait."

DaVinci responds, "No, Mr. Giocondo. I am not that kind of man."

LATER THAT WEEK, DAVINCI AND ONE OF THE BASILICA monks are pulling a two-wheeled hand cart toward the entrance to the Ospedale degli Innocenti. The cart is made of crude wood but tricked out with colorful, nautilus-type pinwheels covering the actual spokes. Every time the cart moves, the pinwheels take a spin of rainbow joy. The cart is piled high with all manner of art supplies; from canvas, brushes and framing material to chalk, paper and paint.

The same two nuns who were previously with Lisa happily come outside to greet the men.

Nun #1 says, "More supplies for our little artistes, Mr. DaVinci?"

"To clear the excess around me is to clear my mind for what lies ahead," explains DaVinci.

The monk complains, "Too much, too messy, too heavy, Sister."

"He seems most comfortable with lifting prayers than lifting heavy objects," says DaVinci, with a wink.

"Follow me," instructs, Nun #2. "Into what we call the hospital's own children's studio."

DaVinci and the monk pull the cart down a hall into the same room where Lisa had emptied her trunk. They all start taking the contents out of the cart, when DaVinci notices the handmade birds that dangle from the ceiling on colorful ribbons.

"Tell me about this heavenly art installation, Sister. It is delightful." DaVinci remarks.

"La Gioconda," answers Nun #2.

"Mona Lisa made every bird by hand," continues Nun #1, proudly. "We took turns climbing a ladder. And raised the whole flock by ourselves."

"The children must enjoy the birds in flight above them," says the monk. "It is a true form of optimistic healing to look up."

DaVinci continues to look up. "Yes it is, Brother. Yes it is."

THE NEXT DAY, DAVINCI IS IN HIS OFFICE / LIBRARY WITH Giocondo and Lisa. There are drawings spread out everywhere and several of the larger codices open for close study.

"I thought she was sitting for you today," Giocondo says to DaVinci.

"All in good time," DaVinci says. "First, I must take you both through the process."

Giocondo, eager to get going, looks very displeased. Lisa

looks relieved, and says,

"To be honest, Leo, I would never have agreed to sit for a portrait. But Francesco said you agreed to include some sketches of our baby in heaven. How could I say no."

When DaVinci shoots Giocondo a puzzled look, Giocondo quickly feigns great interest in an open codex.

The silent exchange between the men loudly tells Lisa her husband was lying.

Lisa says, "Our baby girl was named Francesca. Her first word was papa. She had a crown of curls her papa would never let me cut."

To change the subject entirely, Giocondo asks, "What animal is this, Maestro?"

DaVinci points in the codex at a specific drawing. "This is just one of the many drawings for The Lady with an Ermine. Drawings are the initial part of the process."

Lisa comes over to look at the drawing. Giocondo, perplexed, scratches his head and asks, "What the hell is an ermine?"

"A weasel," answers Lisa. "Very sharp claws and pointy teeth."

"So says Lisa, the farm girl," comments Giocondo.

She adds, "Weasels attack anything that moves. Mice, rabbits, owls, even birds of prey. They are cute and soft but fast and fierce. I saw one kill a rooster in a minute. Terrible."

"Yet there is a positive trait, Mr. Giocondo," says DaVinci. "It is documented that the ermine would rather die than soil itself." Giocondo looks like he's about to hurl.

DaVinci continues, "That animal was one of the most well-behaved subjects I have ever had the pleasure to paint. He would sit for hours without moving a muscle. Which is more than I can say for the lady."

"When did you start working on that portrait," asks Giocondo.

"There may be a date on one of the drawings," answers DaVinci.

Giocondo and Lisa search through a few drawings: the ermine's claws, the ermine's face, the lady's face, the lady's hand, etc.

Lisa, happy with a discovery says, "I found a date, 1489."

"When did you finish?" Giocondo asks DaVinci.

DaVinci answers, "I was still working out the details in 1491."

Gicondo responds, "Two years for such an insignificant little thing."

"This portrait measures 54 centimeters by 39 centimeters (21"× 15 ") Mr. Giocondo. But there is nothing insignificant about it," states DaVinci.

"Yes, She is a true noblewoman. Regal. A fine lady of manners," observes Lisa.

"She is Cecillia Gallerani. Mistress of Ludovico Sforza. Duke of Milan," says DaVinci.

"How much did he pay?" wonders Giocondo.

Lisa quips, "For the portrait or the mistress."

"Think that's funny, Lisa? You stupid assassina," responds Giocondo. He looks like he's about to hit his wife. "Assassin."

DaVinci explains, "I am showing you The Lady with an Ermine as an example of my process and timeline. I start by studying her posture and the precise way she sits. The way she is dressed. The way the ermine is placed in her lap. Her hair. Her wardrobe. Her right hand. His front paws. I created a codex filled with drawings like those you just saw."

"When I am close to being satisfied with one particular

drawing," DaVinci continues, "she will sit for me again, so I can proceed to paint the portrait on canvas. When I am close to satisfied with the portrait on canvas, she again will sit for me so I can proceed to paint the portrait on wood. I apply the gesso. Then, I underdraw before applying my own mix of pigments with oil. "And," DaVinci emphasizes, "We haven't yet discussed how stringent I am about the choice of background paint and design. Which can be the most important and time-consuming elements in the entire process. Period."

"I had no idea," says Lisa, surprised.

"I will follow the process with Mona Lisa," DaVinci says. "I will also follow the process with The Battle of Anghiari. Simultaneously. Drawing in codex to drawing on wall."

Silence as DaVinci organizes the drawings and closes all the codices that were open.

"No teeth," says Giocondo, "I didn't see either animal with teeth."

"It would have been quite difficult for me to remind the ermine to show his teeth," says DaVinci. "And more than a bit dangerous for all involved."

"Speaking of teeth," says Giocondo, "Whatever potion you gave my wife has started to do wonders."

Lisa nods, DaVinci smiles.

"Of course, the fact that I forbade any sweets or sugar in our home was ultimately the contributing factor," Giocondo brags.

"Well, this is my home, Mr. Giocondo," says DaVinci. "And this is the pineapple you gave me to serve." DaVinci produces a tray with pineapple slices perfectly arranged in concentric circles. "Help yourself, Lisa."

Later in DaVinci's studio, Lisa stands by the chair wearing a simple, yet elegant cloak. DaVinci, again on the wooden stool, picks up a large codex. Giocondo is opening a box.

"I was wondering what was in that box sent here from your workshop," says DaVinci. "Perhaps more coffee and pineapple, Mr Giocondo?"

Giocondo smiles and shakes his head. DaVinci opens the codex.

"Lisa, would you be comfortable sitting in front of me wearing only your linen chemise?" asks DaVinci. "I can draw your musculature more accurately that way."

Lisa takes a deep breath, nods, removes her cloak and sits in the chair facing DaVinci. Her head is down her hands are clenched.

"You dirty old man," teases Giocondo.

DaVinci replies, "Never has a more false phrase been spoken, Mr. Giocondo. Now, Lisa. Please turn directly toward me," he continues. She does. "Now a slight turn to your right." She does that, too. "Please unclench those talented hands of yours, my dear."

"You call my hands talented, Leo?" Lisa asks.

"I have some very reliable sources," DaVinci teases.

"Talented my ass," replies Giocondo.

"A talented ass can serve to delight many of us, Mr. Giocondo," responds DaVinci. "Now, Lisa. Tip your lovely chin up." She does. "Tip your chin down." She does. "A bit too much, Lisa. Relax. Be natural." She does what he asks. "Perfetta," he says. She nods.

Giocondo walks toward Lisa carrying a pile of fabric he's taken out of the box. "Oh, Maestro," suggests Giocondo. "Let us skip to the wardrobe part of the process, shall we?"

Piece by piece, fabric by sumptuous fabric, Giocondo begins dramatically draping his wife, shoulder to shoulder, toe to toe. "Perfetta," he exclaims.

DaVinci asks, "How do you feel, Lisa?"

"Itchy," she whispers.

"Sit there and deal with it, assassina," orders Giocondo.

DaVinci asks her, "Would you like to take a break?" Stoically, she shakes her head.

"Honestly, Mr. Giocondo," calmly says DaVinci, "I believe the most beautiful part of any woman is her sternoclavicular."

"You are a dirty old man," accuses Giocondo.

DaVinci puts down the codex, stands up and slowly walks to Lisa. Gently, he lowers the fabric over her left shoulder to reveal the skeletal joint in question.

"Beauty where the shoulder joins the clavicle, Mr. Giocondo," says DaVinci.

"My apologies," responds Giocondo. "You can't possibly be dirty if you believe that is the most beautiful part of a woman's body." He pulls the fabric down further to reveal the top of her breast. "This is."

The three of them are silent. Giocondo smiles. DaVinci, horrified, shakes his head. Lisa, gathering all her self-respect, rises up while removing the entire length of fabric Giocondo has wrapped around her. Standing with defiance in her unadorned linen chemise, she finds her cloak, puts it back on and leaves.

DaVinci says sternly, "I would like to have a talk with your wife. Where did she go?"

Giocondo responds, "Ask a monk. Any monk."

THE PRIVATE GIOCONDO CHAPEL IS NEARLY AS IMPRESSIVE as the rest of the basilica. Soaring stained glass windows feature the many joys and tribulations of the blessed Virgin Mary. The altar is adorned with all things gold, silver, and precious stones.

Lisa sits in one of the long pews, saying a silent prayer – probably to deliver her from Francesco Giocondo.

DaVinci enters and sits in the same pew a respectful distance from Lisa. He looks around at the chapel environment.

He is shocked by the gigantic round symbols of the wool guild and the silk guild hanging on the chapel wall next to many priceless religious objects.

DaVinci, pointing at the symbols, comments, "Interesting mix of secular and religious."

Lisa, head down, answers with a single word. "Offensive."

DaVinci nods his head, saying, "Obviously not to the Giocondo family." He moves a bit closer to Lisa in the pew. She moves a bit closer to him. "What I find offensive, Lisa," he continues, "is a husband who calls his wife assassina."

"Term of endearment," Lisa says, emotionless.

"It means murderer, Lisa," says DaVinci.

"I am aware of that, Leo," says Lisa.

"Did you kill somebody?" asks DaVinci, softly.

She looks at DaVinci and says, "Not that I know of."

"Then why?"

"When Francesco first saw me, I was on the ground trying to soothe a fatally injured calf who was being put to sleep. Maybe he thought I killed it," rationalizes Lisa.

"How old were you?"

"Fourteen. The oldest of seven children living on one of our farms in Chianti," says Lisa. "We grew wheat, made wine and olive oil - raised livestock. Once upon a time, the Gherardini's were among the well-respected families living like nobility in Florence."

Lisa continues, "My mother had passed, leaving my father with seven children and at least that many mortgages. Meanwhile, the del Giocondo family became much richer and more successful than my family could ever be. My father grew more and more desperate.

I was the obvious scapegoat."

"That doesn't explain assassina," says DaVinci. "You must have a reckoning with your husband, Lisa."

"I can't," she says, quietly.

"Why?" says DaVinci, confused.

"It would kill him," she says, definitively.

DaVinci takes Lisa's hand. "I suggest the long way back to the studio," he says.

They walk out of the private chapel through the magnificent basilica toward the main exit.

"I want you to see something, Lisa." DaVinci stops in front of Bartolomeo's Annunciation. "One of the Servite monks painted this three centuries ago," DaVinci continues.

"I walked past the painting hundreds of times. But I never stopped to look," said Lisa.

DaVinci continues, "That is a common oversight. The artwork just becomes part of the furniture as they say. Without study, no one can really appreciate how Bartolomeo captured the weight of that moment. When angel Gabriel announces to Mary that she is pregnant by God with the Son of God. Look at her hands, Lisa. Can you describe them?"

Lisa leans in as close as possible. She tries long and hard to focus on the Virgin's hands. "Her hands are beautiful," Lisa says.

"What else?" DaVinci asks.

"Her hands are folded in her lap. Not clenched. Relaxed," says Lisa, surprised. "How is that possible?"

"If our Holy Queen can calmly sit in front of an angel announcing that newsflash, you can calmly sit in front of DaVinci. With your hands relaxed. Not clenched," he says.

Lisa nods her head. They continue walking together through the basilica's heavy doors.

"I would like to hear more about baby Francesca," says DaVinci.

DAVINCI HAS RETURNED TO HIS STUDIO AND IS SORTING out a pile of correspondence. There is a knock from outside the bookcase door. DaVinci opens the door and sees Giocondo.

"I didn't think you would let me in, Maestro," says Giocondo, sheepishly.

"I shouldn't," DaVinci coldly answers.

"I want to apologize for my behavior." Giocondo enters.

"Apologize to your wife, Mr Giocondo," DaVinci says without sympathy. "I don't allow cruelty in my office, in my studio or in my workshop. Anywhere around me for that matter.

DaVinci continues, "That behavior is very unbecoming to a man of your stature and great influence. I expect it from a particular artist I will soon be forced to work with. Not you."

"There is something you don't know about our relationship, Maestro," Giocondo admits. "So painful, Lisa and I have avoided the issue for a very long time."

"I will not get involved in your relationship. I will not get involved in any relationship, including my own," DaVinci says.

Giocondo laughs a bit, smiles and asks, "Is Lisa still here?"

"I offered her my carriage. She left and took the box of fabrics with her," answers DaVinci. "But, as you are still here, I want to show you something."

DaVinci opens another large codex, flips a few pages and points. Giocondo's eyes nearly bulge out of their sockets.

"The Battle of Anghiari, my final rendering of what will soon appear on the East wall.

This is a much smaller version, of course," says DaVinci. "The mural will be enormous. Please inform the committee, Mr. Giocondo, that I will be using encausto, my revolutionary technique. By applying a wax to the rough, ancient plaster, I can insure better adherence of oil paint pigment in whatever colors I choose. Muted. Murky. Malevolent."

Giocondo isn't listening. "I have never seen such violence. Soldiers on horses. Swirling like wild, rabid dogs tearing each other apart. Yet one soldier appears the most fierce. Me."

DaVinci asks, "Remember? You were in my studio posing with a chest plate and helmet." Giocondo nods, his eyes affixed to the page. "I drew your face from memory." DaVinci says. "Obviously, I managed to capture the essence."

"Would you give me that helmet, Maestro?" asks a childlike Giocondo.

DaVinci responds, "I would not, Mr. Giocondo. I may want someone else to wear it."

THAT NIGHT, THE UNHAPPY COUPLE ARE IN THEIR MASTER bedroom with chaises and armoires reminiscent of Versailles. Lisa is tucked into one twin bed. With a long bureau between them, Giocondo is tucked into another. Moonlight streams in through glass balcony doors.

Lisa asks quietly. "Are you awake?"

No response.

"Francesco?" Lisa repeats, a bit louder.

"I am awake now, Lisa," Giocondo responds, angry.

"Assassina," she says.

"What about it," he says.

"You can never call me that," she demands. "Ever again,"

"DaVinci. He told you to say that to me?" Giocondo asks.

"No," says Lisa.

"Well, he told me to say it." Giocondo adds. "So, yes. Because I want that portrait hanging at eye level in the foyer, I will seriously consider not calling you assassina."

"Thank you, Frankie," Lisa says, relieved.

"Even though you are," he says bluntly.

EARLY THE NEXT MORNING, DaVINCI HAS RETURNED TO the children's studio in the foundling hospital. He is lying prone on one of the long table benches, looking straight up at the flock of handmade birds that dangle from the ceiling on colorful ribbons. Nun #2 enters.

The nun asks him quietly. "Are you awake?"

No response. She finds a ruler, picks it up, smiles and gently taps his head.

"DaVinci," the nun repeats, a bit louder. "Are you awake?"

"I am gazing at the flock of birds above me, Sister." DaVinci responds. "Every child in Florence should have the same gazing opportunity."

"Why stop at Florence," says the nun, seriously.

DaVinci sits up and puts his hands on the table. The nun sits across from him.

"How was your examination?" asks the nun. "I know the appointment was scheduled for this morning."

"The doctors were vague. The medical students were clear," DaVinci tells her.

"Is there a diagnosis?" the nun asks.

"Yes," DaVinci says with reluctance. He picks up a piece of chalk and starts drawing on a random piece of paper. "My left hand is as it should be."

"That wasn't the reason you were here at 6 am," she says.

"Every doctor, every medical student has been sworn to secrecy. The monks, as well,"

DaVinci explains. "So must you be."

"As novices, we take a vow of silence," she says. "Nuns are trained to keep secrets secret. But I am sure you could also trust our dear Mona Lisa."

He says, "Lisa will find out eventually. The disease is degenerative. It will get worse."

DaVinci uses his left hand to demonstrate on his right arm. "The ulnar nerve travels down from shoulder to hand, controlling movement and feeling. A past injury, a fall, even a repetitive motion can cause damage beyond repair. The diagnosis? Ulnar nerve palsy. First weakening, then destroying the muscles that allow me to make fine movements. With my fingers. God forbid Michelangelo finds out."

DaVinci drums his right-hand fingers on the table. Nun #2 covers his hand with hers.

THE NEXT DAY, DaVINCI TRIES DESPERATELY TO MAKE progress drawing Lisa's portrait. Again, she sits only wearing her linen chemise. Giocondo, in even more obnoxious form, is suggesting piece after piece of jewelry. He puts a heavy necklace on Lisa, then stands back to judge how it looks. DaVinci, the same large codex in his lap, quickly draws the necklace on his subject.

Giocondo shakes his head. DaVinci tears the drawing out of the codex, crumples it up and throws it on the floor.

Giocondo puts a garish tiara on Lisa's head, stands back to judge how it looks. As DaVinci draws the tiara on his subject, Lisa confidently shakes her head, removes the tiara and hands it back to Giocondo. Like a robot, DaVinci tears that drawing out of the codex, crumples it up and throws it on the floor.

Giocondo puts several bracelets on both of Lisa's wrists. DaVinci draws the bracelets on his subject. Giocondo stands back, wrinkles his brow and adds more bracelets. DaVinci draws that iteration, too. When Giocondo adds even more bracelets. DaVinci finally loses his patience and throws the entire codex on the floor.

"I have been beyond tolerant with your wealth of suggestions," Mr. Giocondo. "And we are not even close to the point where wardrobe must be selected and finalized."

"I so look forward to that," says Giocondo with a smile.

"As do I," says Lisa with a frown.

"To keep you up to date on scheduling, I have been approved by the committee to begin my battle in The Hall Of The Five Hundred."

Lisa applauds. Giocondo applauds, then stops abruptly. He suddenly seems concerned.

"Does that mean you will not be working on my portrait?" Giocondo asks.

"My portrait," Lisa corrects.

"Still my portrait," DaVinci responds.

"The process may be slower," says DaVinci. "But as you know, I draw with my left hand and paint with my right. However, Mr. Giocondo. If you stop interfering with the artist, the artist can do what the artist does. And do it to the very best of his ability."

"I am entitled to my opinion, Sir," Giocondo says defensively.

"Enough," comments Lisa.

"Enough out of you." answers Giocondo.

"I am growing older as we speak," says DaVinci. "I want to establish your final pose, Lisa. Your wardrobe, with all its certain controversy, will have to wait. Weeks."

"I know a stall tactic when I hear one," Giocondo says.

"There is a meeting of the wool guild I am already late for," says Giocondo. "Please contact me when I can return to choose Lisa's dress and hairstyle and footwear."

"This portrait is a three quarter composition. Her feet will never appear." DaVinci says.

"So." says Giocondo with attitude. "I will choose her footwear."

Giocondo struts out. Lisa stands up, stretches and sits down. DaVinci does the same. Lisa assumes her final pose. DaVinci picks up his codex and draws in earnest. They sit there like that for quite some time. DaVinci puts down his codex, stands and leaves. Lisa doesn't move. In minutes, DaVinci returns with a tray filled with goodies and juices. Lisa stands and puts a long vest over her linen chemise.

"I think we both deserve refreshments," says DaVinci.

"You are sooooo right," answers Lisa, pointing to the tray. "Is that what I hope it is?"

"Nougat from the south of France?" DaVinci teases. "Yes, Mona Lisa. Your wish. Granted."

DaVinci puts the tray down at a makeshift table and finds two rickety stools. They sit, eat and drink with gusto. DaVinci starts a conversation. "One of the basilica monks and I delivered a cartful of art supplies to the Ospedale degli Innocenti.

"Very kind and generous of you," comments Lisa.

"Not really. A purge was necessary to clear my creative path," answers DaVinci. "We wheeled the cart into what the nuns call their children's studio. You are familiar with that room, correto?"

Lisa nods her head and drinks a large glass of peach juice.

"The uccelli," DaVinci comments. "The handmade birds that dangle from the ceiling on colorful ribbons. You hand made them?" DaVinci pours himself a glass of orange juice.

"When I was growing up, my brothers, sisters and I raised homing pigeons," says Lisa.

It is many years ago. A young Lisa and her younger siblings are on a roof with a wooden coop filled with noisy pigeons ready for flight. The siblings each take a bird and release it with glee.

Lisa cradles one small bird with an injured wing that is bandaged and splinted to its body.

She strokes the bird's head and gently removes the bandage and splint. The bird joyfully flaps both wings and coos at Lisa with thanks.

Lisa picks up the bird and walks to the edge of the roof.

She looks at the bird. The bird looks at her. With a deep breath, Lisa releases it.

The bird flies higher and higher, then disappears.

Everyone waits not so patiently for their own homing pigeons to come home. Ten minutes pass. One by one, the pigeons return to the children's delight. Lisa, eyes to the sky, waits longer. Ten minutes, twenty minutes, an hour. Her bird never comes back.

"THAT IS HOW I FEEL EVERY DAY," SAYS LISA, SADLY. "I CAN never go home. I am uncomfortable in my own home. I want to fly away with a flock of uccelli. And never come back."

"I have a business proposition for you, Lisa," states DaVinci.

"I am not a businessman, Leo." she responds.

"You can be a businesswoman, Lisa," he answers. "Not for profit. For the children. We can even trick your husband to making a material contribution of wools and silks. That is the kind of charity to build good will everywhere he does business."

"You want me to make a business out of making uccelli?" Lisa asks, unconvinced. "I couldn't sew that many birds in a lifetime."

"There is space in the Ospedale degli Innocenti," explains DaVinci. The entire basement, in fact. You and a team could work under the watchful portrait of Giocondo's brother. Rent free."

"Team? I don't have a team, Leo," she says.

"I've already done a little recruiting for you, Lisa," he tells her. "The nuns, some of my apprentices, most of the students I've been teaching at the art academy, maybe even some of the guild weavers. They would all volunteer to help create your uccelli."

"I would want to pay them somehow."

"That will not be an issue, Lisa. I have the support of a pope, a poet, a duke, a king and a Medici," he says. "To sew and sell what I have named The Uccellisa."

Lisa responds, "Uccellisa. Only Leondardo DaVinci could invent a name like that."

DaVinci holds out his hand to Lisa. They heartily shake hands.

MONTHS PASS. BUT THE TRIUMVIRATE HAS FINALLY reunited in DaVinci's studio. He looks tired, thinner and greyer. Lisa looks strong. Giocondo looks more prosperous if that's even possible. Gicondo rubs his hands together with the greatest expectation.

"At long last, wardrobe," announces Giocondo. "It's taken eons, Maestro."

"I'm busy. You're busy. And Lisa is the busiest of all," says DaVinci, happily.

"I'm proud of everyone helping The Uccellisa. Which has really taken off," Lisa quips.

"All my customers, especially all the new customers," Giocondo emphasizes, "buy more wool and silk when they learn of my material contribution to charity. "Of course, Maestro," adds Giocondo, "your participation gives a level of credibility and status that cannot be bought."

"La Gioconda is delighting all the children," says DaVinci like a proud uncle. "And encouraging them to keep looking up. I hope we will be as delighted with her wardrobe."

Lisa, wearing her linen chemise, is steeled for the decision. Giocondo gleefully rubs his hands yet again. DaVinci walks to the rack where many long dresses are hanging, pressed and ready.

"You will be trying one dress after another," states DaVinci. "This does not have to be a big drama or a competition. Each one of us wants the same thing. An elegant, original, high-end look that no other woman can own or wear as well as Mona Lisa. I will choose first."

"I will choose first," says Giocondo.

"Fine," says DaVinci. "I am too tired to argue."

Giocondo hands Lisa one dress after another after another. He nods enthusiastically after every dress, while DaVinci and Lisa simply shake their heads. Giocondo's choice of dresses are too extravagant, too brightly colored, too fitted, too formal, too too.

"Why do we need a unanimous decision? I should decide. I am the expert," whines Giocondo.

"You may be the fabric expert; perhaps not the fashion expert," says DaVinci.

DaVinci hands Lisa one dress after another after another. He nods enthusiastically after every dress, while Giocondo and Lisa simply shake their heads. DaVinci's choice of dresses are too modest, too granny, too drab, too baggy, too boring.

"You may be the artistic expert, but your style is not of this century," says Giocondo.

"I have one more dress that I am confident we can all agree upon," says DaVinci.

"If not, I will wear this little linen chemise and call it a day," bemoans Lisa.

DaVinci carefully hands Lisa his final choice like it's a priceless and precious treasure.

She puts it on and a hush comes over the studio. It is a simple shift in a deep color made of luxurious silk, loosely pleated at the neck to highlight her face. The exquisite lace work that has been painstakingly added is as subtle as the gold detail in the fold of her arm. Lisa is beaming.

"Please sit for me, Lisa," DaVinci asks. She does, like a queen.

"Where did you find this dress, Maestro?" Giocondo asks.

"With full disclosure, Mr. Giocondo," informs DaVinci, "It was sent to me by Maestro Deluca.

"He chose the fabric and the trim. One of your premiere designers created it for you. All in favor, raise your right hand." They raise their right hands in unison, then Giocondo lowers his.

"Wait. Did you put something on her head?" asks Giocondo.

"A delicate veil, Mr. Giocondo," DaVinci says. "You may not have noticed it covering the lady's head in The Lady with an Ermine."

"I can barely feel it," remarks Lisa. "Yet I somehow feel it shimmer."

"Historically, the veil is worn as a symbol of virtue," explains DaVinci.

"Odd that you painted The Lady with an Ermine wearing one," Giocondo says. "Considering her duty to the duke." Giocondo laughs loud because he is the master of Renaissance sarcasm.

DaVinci walks toward his military table, chooses an object and returns. He walks to Lisa and puts the helmet on her head. She sits there, uncomfortable. DaVinci waits a minute to remove the helmet. He tames Lisa's hair and re-arranges the veil.

"I receive your message loud and clear, Maestro," says Giocondo. "But allow me to add one simple accessory to complete the picture."

Giocondo searches and finds a gossamer scarf on the rack near the dresses. More determined than ever, he struts to Lisa and softly drapes the scarf over her left shoulder.

DaVinci sighs and says, very reluctantly, "Perfetto." "Let us now celebrate our unanimous wardrobe decision with a cup of freshly-ground coffee," suggests DaVinci.

"Where did you find coffee beans?" asks a skeptical Giocondo.

"In Venice, Mr. Giocondo," says DaVinci. "Trans-Oceanic trade routes and all that."

A monk enters with a tray of three steaming cups of coffee, plus bowls of cream and sugar.

"Hot," the monk warns. He carefully puts down the tray and says, "Blow." He starts to leave, but turns around and announces to Lisa, "We have sold three dozen Uccellisa today." He leaves.

"Three dozen sold. Coffee with sugar." Lisa says. "I am a happy woman."

WEEKS LATER AT DUSK, DAVINCI IS IN HIS MODEST bedroom, removing his clothing drenched in heavy sweat and paint. Every time he moves his right arm, he winces and cries out in agony. Finally, he is shirtless.

On a dresser in containers and bowls are various plants, herbs, and flowers. He finds one very large bowl, then fills it with a variety of ingredients. Although it causes even more pain, he crushes the ingredients together, continuing until the plants, herbs and flowers are finely compressed.

He searches for bottles of natural oils and mixes those liquids into the large bowl. With both hands, he mixes and mixes and mixes until a creamy paste is formed. He smells the mixture, smiles and nods his head.

He takes the bowl with him to a large chair by a window and sits. Expertly, he uses his left hand to apply the healing cream, all the way down from his right shoulder to his right hand. He uses more cream to massage his fingers, one by one. With every finger he inhales as deeply as possible.

"Mary, my mother, Mary. You have taken me into your house of worship and into your care. Teach me to understand my suffering and endure it with your grace. And give me strength to stretch this canvas on my journey to paint a portrait of your deserving daughter, Mona Lisa. Amen."

With incredible fortitude, DaVinci puts on a clean muslin tunic and walks into a small studio next door. After lighting some lanterns to illuminate the room, he finds four pieces of pre-measured, pre-cut wood, brings them to a worktable and nails them into a frame with a hammer.

Exhausted, he pauses for a moment and says to himself, "Which battle is worth fighting, Leo. The one on the wall or the one on the easel?" He stands slowly and rubs his right arm from shoulder to hand. He goes about finding pieces of linen canvas; also pre-measured and pre-cut.

DaVinci puts one piece of canvas on the table, then puts the wooden frame on top of the canvas. He finds a box of small nails and puts several in his mouth. With the hammer in his right hand, he takes one nail of his mouth and bangs the nail through the canvas into the frame, screaming. He puts the hammer in his left hand, repeating the process until the canvas is stretched tight on the frame.

Finally, he prepares the canvas by applying a light coat of fluid glue. Again, to himself,

"Take time to dry, my canvas friend. I will take that time to dine on cook's pesto masterpiece."

ALL SENIOR MEMBERS OF THE WOOL GUILD AND THE SILK guild have been told to gather in one of the grand auditoriums of Florence at daybreak the next morning. People are buzzing and questions are flying. The crowd is filled with anticipation of who-knows-what-is-to-come.

There is silence as Francesco Giocondo strides to the podium like a charismatic combination of Brad Pitt and Benito Mussolini. He wears a long, dark velvet tunic, with a light blue ceremonial sash draped from shoulder to hip. The sash is fastened by a gold medal so big, it could have been seen with the refracting telescope DaVinci was building in his workshop. (Yes, before Galileo.)

Giocondo reaches the podium, turns to the audience and lifts his arms as a signal for applause. Everyone does, with grande entusiasmo. Giocondo bows, then lowers his arms as a signal for quiet. A pin drop could be heard, probably from one of several tailors in attendance.

Giocondo clears his throat, then says, "I want to thank you for showing up at sunrise to hear a very important announcement. As the most senior members of the wool guild and the silk guild, it is your responsibility to share this news with those who work with you and for you. In the next month or so, I will travel to Rome. I have travelled to Rome many times, as you know. But this trip is the most significant. Not only for the Giocondo family, but for every one of you."

"I, as the esteemed Consul of the Guilds, have been contacted by the Vatican. To supply enough silk and wool to recreate not only the vestments for the pontiff himself, but his monsignors, his bishops, his cardinals and even the flamboyant uniforms worn by Swiss mercenaries stationed there to guard the Holy See." Giocondo raises his arms again. Thunderous applause ensues.

"This opportunity can change everything. From increasing your workload to exalting your status. As Consul, I realize how dedicated you are to the guild. I respect your integrity, your ability and, above all, your generosity to the children of Florence.

"We are all volunteers in the charitable production and distribution of the hand made birds that dangle from the ceiling on colorful ribbons. My contribution has been to supply any and all fabric to make the children happy. I will continue that supply, no matter how large the quantity will be.

But I cannot continue allowing my guild members to waste any work hours for hands-on participation with those birds. Participation on private time? Your decision, of course. But that time must be reported to me. Accurately and consistently."

Thank you for your attendance this morning. And thank you for listening."

The audience is stunned as Giocondo strides out. No one dare say a word about the blunt message he has just delivered.

Yet one face in the crowd says it all. DeLuca. If looks could kill, the result would certainly be the demise of Francesco Giocondo. With the giant gold medal deeply embedded in his neck.

MANY MONTHS LATER, DAVINCI AND LISA ARE IN HIS studio. Slowly, progress has been made. Lisa is posed, wardrobed and comfortable. DaVinci sits on his wooden stool now with two cushions. He is painting on a canvas resting on an easel in front of him. There is a palette of different color paints on a small table next to him. He tightly holds a small paintbrush in his right hand.

"We do not have the pleasure of your husband's input today, Lisa?" asks DaVinci.

"I'm sure he'll be barging in soon enough," Lisa answers. "Unless he's too busy chastising some of the weavers still volunteering after hours on The Uccellisa."

DaVinci dips his brush into the palette and painstakingly adds to a partially painted version of Mona Lisa. "Mr. Giocondo is suffering," comments DaVinci. "I believe his pain comes from a profound psychological wound buried within."

"You are a man filled with forgiveness, Leo," says Lisa. "I am empty."

DaVinci picks up another brush and dips it into another color. "It has taken my entire life to forgive my father," DaVinci says. "He never really acknowledged my existence, let alone the latent talent I exhibited even as a young boy."

"Your mother?" Lisa asks.

DaVinci explains, "My father's wife was not my mother. A respected notary, he paid many peasant women for favors they would willingly provide. I was born from one of those favors. My mother ignored the dalliance and the delivery. Women were expected to look the other way."

"They still are," agrees Lisa.

Giocondo strides into the studio. He carries several long rolls of canvas and leans then against the wall. Silent, he stands behind DaVinci, then starts a critical commentary. "The quality of that canvas is inferior. I can clearly see the crosshatch weave on every single brushstroke."

"Hello, Francesco," Lisa says.

Ignoring his wife, Giocondo continues his criticism. "Her posture is off, your shadows are wrong and the measurement of the canvas is too small for such an important work."

DaVinci puts his brush down and turns to Giocondo. "Nice to see you, Mr. Giocondo. Of course," DaVinci continues. "I always consider your multitude of comments."

"I have explained to you, ad infinitum," he continues, "that this canvas and another to follow, represent the step after my final drawing, and the step before painting the final portrait on wood. You agreed to the steps in my process, as well as the precise measurement of the portrait itself."

"I did not agree that the first canvas would take well over a year," says Giocondo. "Yet you started painting in the Hall of The Five Hundred months ago."

DaVinci answers, "I went directly from the drawings approved by the committee to painting. Think about it, Mr. Giocondo. Covering the East wall with canvas on which to experiment would be absurd…no matter how much help my apprentices or my students could offer."

Lisa finally pipes up. "Leo. Did you just call my husband absurd?"

Giocondo kicks the rolls of canvas onto the floor. "Fine.

Use canvas that looks like what an ermine holds in, instead of the linen I specially sourced for you in Venice," says Giocondo. "And, Maestro? Try painting a smile on that face. So she does not appear to be a poor, sad, ugly victim of some low-life, medieval wife beater." He struts out.

Quietly, DaVinci says to Lisa, "That went well."

Lisa responds, "At least Francesco didn't use his political clout to bankrupt The Uccellisa.

And deprive so many other children from joyfully looking up."

"Mr. Giocondo is threatened by your success," says DaVinci.

"My husband would not even be threatened by Hannibal riding an elephant," says Lisa.

DaVinci laughs, "Not if the elephant remembers the power and potential of its own velocity. Now. Instead of watching paint dry, we will enjoy a brief expedition. Then return for more painting, Mona Lisa. Hang up your dress and put a long cloak over your chemise. I will become incognito."

She asks, "Expedition. To where?"

He says, "Where we will join a crowd of other people joyfully looking up."

An exuberant crowd has gathered and everyone is looking up in unison.

Wearing a hooded black robe borrowed from one of the monks, DaVinci is completely unrecognizable. With Lisa on his arm, the two of them blend seamlessly into the crowd.

DaVinci studies everyone carefully, to make sure Michelangelo is not among them.

Because, on this pivotal expedition, DaVinci has brought Lisa to see a seventeen-foot-tall statue of David: the future king and recently bar-mitzvahed slayer of Goliath, the Philistine giant, both memorialized in the Book of Samuel.

"Amazing what a slovenly sculptor hath wrought from a discarded slab of marble," DaVinci comments. "Yet nowhere in the bible or any artwork or any description is young David devoid of any clothing. Slingshot, yes. Bare naked, no."

DaVinci and Lisa don't talk with one another during their entire time with David.

They walk around the statue, they stop to look up.

They continue to walk, they stop to look up.

They walk around the statue in the opposite direction, they stop to look up.

They get as close to David as possible for another perspective.

They move far away from David for another perspective.

They silently leave the noisy crowd.

No one looked at DaVinci, because no one was looking anywhere but up.

BACK IN THE STUDIO AFTER THEIR EXPEDITION, LISA IS putting on her wardrobe dress. DaVinci sits at the easel, having returned the black hooded robe to its rightful religious owner.

As Lisa sits down to re-strike her pose, DaVinci dips his brush into water, then into paint. He taps off the excess liquid and holds his brush near the canvas, trying hard to steady his right hand.

Lisa is immobile as DaVinci starts to paint another part of her portrait on the canvas. "I sent Buonarrati the finest case of vintage Amarone weeks ago when David was unveiled," says DaVinci. "I included a one-word note that said 'Masterpiece!' with an exclamation mark. Yet I believe his masterpiece is flawed. Most people will see David as a grown man, not a teenage boy. His hands are grotesque and out of proportion. The statue has a static musculature devoid of any tension that should foreshadow the boy's action to come. I am curious, Lisa. What do you think?"

She lowers her head almost imperceptibly. DaVinci pauses and takes his brush from the canvas. "Lisa?" he asks again. She lifts her head and looks at him honestly.

Her reaction is the infamous Mona Lisa smile, a mystery no longer.

"Lisa!" exclaims DaVinci. "That is the smile I have been waiting for. But let it be a secret how your smile came to be. Agreed?"

She nods her head, repeats the subtle smile and says, "Agreed."

Giocondo struts in carrying a small leather bag, "What is the agreement between you two?" he asks. "A bigger portrait? A shorter time frame? A lifetime of sugar cakes?"

Lisa and DaVinci shake their heads simultaneously. Giocondo strides over to the canvas. He checks out the portrait in progress and studies the paints on DaVinci's palette. Giocondo carefully takes a small jar of a dark, thick purple-colored liquid from the leather bag and asks, "Do you know what this is, Maestro?"

"A fluid chromatic of some sort," DaVinci replies.

"Oricello rosso," Giocondo says like a professor. "The purple dye highly valued by the classical Greeks and Romans. The Rucelli family discovered it centuries ago. The Giocondo family perfected it as an effective, non-fading, superior dye for wool. Royal purple and all that. Here."

Giocondo hands the jar to DaVinci who seems puzzled.

"Thank you, Mr. Giocondo," says DaVinci. "But I am not planning to dye any wool fabric in the near future."

"Oh, this dye is not for wool fabric," Giocondo explains. "It is for linen canvas. Perhaps adding a depth of color to the portrait on the easel in front of you."

"My palette is filled with paints I have scientifically mixed with oil for that sole purpose," says DaVinci. "Not only would your oricello rosso not properly adhere to the canvas, Mr. Giocondo, the dye could compromise the paints I have already applied."

Giocondo picks up a paintbrush and tries handing it to DaVinci. The artist shakes his head.

Giocondo tries handing the paintbrush to DaVinci much more forcibly. The artist folds his arms across his chest.

Slowly, Giocondo opens the jar and puts it down next to the palette on the table.

He holds the brush above the jar, poised to dip it into the liquid.

"Francesco," asks Lisa, frightened. "What are you doing?"

Giocondo dips the brush into the liquid. "What does it look like, Lisa?" he says, annoyed.

He taps the brush on the side of the jar to remove the excess of thick liquid.

Without hesitation, he paints a swath of purple directly over Mona Lisa's head. Silence.

The swath says put until it doesn't.

Slowly the liquid seeps deep into the canvas leaving an obvious purple stain.

"Oops," says Giocondo. He puts the brush down, picks up the jar, puts the cover back on, puts the jar back into the bag and struts out.

"He knew exactly what would happen," says Lisa, very angry.

DaVinci says, gently, "I need to concentrate on waging The Battle of Anghiari, Lisa. When we again reunite for the portrait, I know you will remember that wonderfully subtle smile."

NEARLY A YEAR LATER, LISA AND GIOCONDO ARE IN HIS palatial office suite at the silk workshop. They sit far from each other at a long table, not speaking. DeLuca limps into the room using a cane. He has two packages in his left hand. One is large and beautifully wrapped, the other is smaller and wrapped in tissue paper. Lisa jumps up immediately and runs to greet him. Giocondo stays put.

"Mister DeLuca," Lisa exclaims. "So wonderful to see you, sir."

DeLuca responds, "Wonderful to see both of you together. In the same room."

Giocondo agrees, "Same room." Giocondo disagrees, "Together. Not so much."

"But for the same reason, yes?" DeLuca asks.

Giocondo and Lisa nod their heads. Finally, Giocondo stands and pulls out a chair for DeLuca, who puts the packages on the table and sits. They all are seated. No one says a word.

DeLuca starts the conversation. "Terrible. A terrible tragedy."

Lisa says, "Such a sad day for all the citizens of Florence who love and cherish him.

Giocondo says, "He should have known better."

DeLuca, quietly, says, "You have never made a mistake in your life, Francesco?"

Giocondo, looking directly at Lisa, says, "Yes. I made a very big mistake."

DeLuca continues, "Well, Lisa. This might help." He points to the package and says,

"You were so thoughtful to do this."

Lisa explains, "It was Francesco's idea, Mr. DeLuca. I just made a few suggestions."

"Francesco," says Deluca, surprised. "You do have a heart after all."

"Keep that to yourself, Deluca," says Giocondo. "My heart is not for public knowledge."

Ami and Nomi stand by the door and try to peek in. Before Lisa can see them, DeLuca shoos away the red-headed twins as if they were two pesky flies.

DeLuca carefully opens the tissue paper to reveal many long pieces of fabric called auroserici, a rare silk with real gold flowing through the weave like a river of money.

Deluca asks, "This is some of the fabric you chose, yes?"

"Auroserici," Giocondo says.

"The gold is even more beautiful than I remember," comments Lisa.

"I saved the extra yardage for The Uccellisa," DaLuca explains.

"Gold for those damn birds, DeLuca?" Giocondo asks, disgusted.

"Handmade birds that dangle from the ceiling on golden ribbons," says Lisa, proudly.

"Ordered personally by the King of France for every bedroom in the Royal Palace."

"You know I know the Kings of France, Lisa," Giocondo responds.

"And this king will know you supplied auroserici for his palace flock," says Lisa.

"Francesco, say thank you, Lisa," suggests De Luca. "With that big heart of yours."

THAT SAME DAY, LISA AND GIOCONDO QUIETLY WALK INTO DaVinci's studio. Lisa is carrying the beautifully wrapped package. There is no movement, no energy, no art in a space usually filled with life and light. An oversized white floral funeral wreath with black ribbon stands like a sentry, dominating the studio.

DaVinci sits on his two-cushion stool staring at an easel that holds a piece of poplar measuring 77x53 centimeters (30" x 20 7/8"). The wood is completely blank. Dressed like a peasant, he wears a coarse flax shirt, breeches and sandals. His hair and beard are more gray and unkempt.

He looks like a man in defeat.

Lisa and Giocondo walk to DaVinci. "Would you like some company, Leo?" asks Lisa.

"Not really," whispers DaVinci.

"You have no choice in the matter, Maestro." says Giocondo. "Because here we are."

"Mr Giocondo," says DaVinci, "this is definitely not the time to call me Maestro."

"I know what happened, Leo." says Lisa, sympathetically. "I just don't understand why."

Giocondo finds two rickety chairs and drags them over

to DaVinci. Giocondo and Lisa sit next to him. She has the wrapped package on her lap. There is a long, uncomfortable silence until DaVinci speaks. He sounds like a robot in an emotionless, monotone voice. His eyes stay fixed on the blank piece of wood on the easel.

"I finished the East wall. The Battle of Anghiari would finally be documented for the ages.

But, unbeknownst to me, another battle would begin fast and furious. It was hot as hades in The Hall of the Five Hundred. The humidity was equally unbearable. So the paint did not dry and would not dry - leaving the entirety of the mural in jeopardy. So we placed big pots filled with burning wood all along the wall, believing an extreme temperature would quickly dry the painted surface."

DaVinci painfully stretches out his right arm, rubs his right shoulder, gingerly moves his right fingers, takes a deep breath and continues. "The heat of burning wood became so intense so quickly, it melted the wax I had initially applied to the plaster wall. And the paint melted with it."

In their minds, Giocondo and Lisa imagine the artwork dripping down like a Renaissance Jasper Johns or Larry Poons. The soldiers, their weapons, their horses, all gone.

"I saw my punishment rain down before me. Not in dripping paint, but in tears shed for all the battles that did not have to be fought. Tears for innocent citizens as collateral damage. Innocent animals slaughtered or left to carry the soldiers, dead or alive. As a pacifist, this is my cross to bear. The last wall I will ever paint."

Lisa is in tears. Giocondo stands and walks to the easel. He takes a long look at the blank piece of wood and says, "Assuming this will be Mona Lisa's portrait, are you sure I agreed to the size?"

DaVinci looks at him and responds, "Yes, Mr. Giocondo, you agreed."

"Is this walnut wood like you used to paint The Mistress And The Weasel?" Giocondo asks.

DaVinci responds. "No, Mr. Giocondo. It is pristine white poplar. Unblemished. Not one knot."

"You're not going to put any wax on it, I assume," jokes Giocondo.

Everyone laughs and the somber mood of gloom and doom is broken.

"What's with the funeral wreath?" asks Giocondo. "I can smell the white roses from here."

"Guess," answers DaVinci.

Giocondo and Lisa shrug their shoulders. DaVinci points to a large, folded piece of paper on the floor. Giocondo picks it up, unfolds it, reads it and whistles.

The word MASTERPIECE is painted on the paper in watercolor, designed to insure that each letter would dramatically drip down from top to bottom.

Giocondo shows the paper to his wife. Lisa, angry, stands up holding the wrapped package. "He is a disgusting, slob of a man," she says. "Pay no attention, Leo. Focus on this instead."

She hands the package to DaVinci. He struggles to open it, but can't. Giocondo takes the package and opens it with a flourish. He removes the contents and holds it up for DaVinci to see. It is an ankle-length robe sewn of the most luxurious silks and wools. Open in the front with no fasteners, there are twelve vertical panels in twelve different colors; six in the front and six in the back. Each panel is perfectly separated by a trim of gold auroserici. The long sleeves of the robe complete the creation—velvet in a deep magenta. DaVinci is gobsmacked.

"Please put the robe on, Mr Giocondo." DaVinci asks. "So I

can admire its full beauty."

Giocondo is happy to oblige. He puts the robe over his clothing and models it like a pro.

"Lisa, that is the most heartfelt gift I have ever received. From anyone," says DaVinci. "From kings and queens and name a Medici, any Medici."

"I did help choose the gold auroserici, Leo," says Lisa. "But the twelve-panel design and the corresponding colors were all Francesco's doing."

"Don't tell the committee," Giocondo says to DaVinci.

DaVinci, even more shocked, stands up and walks to Giocondo for a closer look.

"I chose the twelve different colors for a reason," says Giocondo, proud of himself.

DaVinci indicates with his index finger that Giocondo demonstrate a full 360° whirl. Giocondo gladly follows the direction to turn turn, turn.

"The Last Supper," DaVinci says softly. "The twelve robes of the twelve apostles and my color choice for each individual robe. And the sleeves, Mr. Giocondo. The sleeves are a near-perfect color match to the robe I painted for Jesus. How did you know that?"

"Francesco works in mysterious ways." answers Lisa. "Most of them behind closed doors."

THE RED-HEADED TWINS ARE IN AN ORDINARY BEDROOM IN an ordinary home. They are rifling through an extraordinary closet filled with fashion of the best materials from the best sources in Europe. They are trying on clothes while having a deep and meaningful conversation. Nomi and Ami pay very careful attention to each other. Nomi shows Ami one dress in particular.

Nomi: Did we already wear this dress?

Ami: I think maybe a year ago. In Milan.

Nomi: The Duomo.

Ami: Ah, the Duomo.

Nomi: It reminded me of a perfectly shaped breast. Like yours.

Ami: Like yours.

Nomi: Like ours.

Ami: Lake Como. So pretty and close to the city.

Nomi: Ah, Lake Como.

Ami: We were supposed to be matching fabric swatches to the robes painted on the wall...

Nomi: ...in the refectory of the Convent of Santa Maria delle Grazie.

Ami: Which we did in a hurry on the way back from Lake Como.

Nomi: Maybe soon the twins will be going to Romo.

They laugh at their own brand of rhyming humor.

Ami: Hmmm. What to wear to meet the pope.

Nomi: Nuns habit.

Ami finds a short black velvet robe, holds it up, shakes her head and throws it on the floor. She finds a long black satin dress and throws it on the floor, as well.

Ami: None of that. This.

Ami finds a conservative dress and shows it to Nomi.

Nomi: Perfetto. A dress LaGioconda would wear.

Ami: But she's not going.

They laugh at LaGioconda's expense.

Nomi: Do we kiss the pope's ring?

Ami: We each kiss the ring and suck his whole finger into our mouth.

Ami pantomimes putting the ring finger of her right hand into her mouth.

Nomi: Then deep, deep down our throat.

Ami: He would like that.

Nomi: He would thank almighty God for being the pope.

They cross themselves, hysterically laughing.

Months later, there is a bit more light and life in DaVinci's studio. Yet the artist himself is still not himself. He sits in his usual place on the cushioned stool in front of the easel. The palette on the table next to him is again full of fresh paint. His right arm is resting on a padded board attached to a mechanism that moves when he moves. This is a system DaVinci designed for more support and less stress while holding a brush and trying to paint every excruciating detail of portraiture.

Lisa, on her chair, in her pose with that smile, sits patiently for DaVinci to put paint on a brush.

The actual Mona Lisa portrait on poplar wood is well on its way. Her body is outlined and her hands are in the process of being painted. Slowly. So painfully slow.

"The people of Florence still look at me with pity," admits DaVinci. "I see it in their eyes."

"Falling down is not a failure. Failure comes when you stay where you have fallen," says Lisa.

"You're quoting Socrates now, Lisa?" says DaVinci,

surprised.

"My father insisted that all seven children be well educated," Lisa explains. 'When the rooster crows, it's time to start reading, he used to say.' The classics were top of his list."

"The 'stay where you have fallen' part of what Socrates meant is incredibly relevant here," says DaVinci. "The reigning French monarch has offered me the title of "Premier Painter, Engineer and Architect to the King," DaVinci continues. "Which may be an offer I can't refuse."

"But your life is here, Leo," says Lisa. "I would be sadly depressed if you left me behind."

"I would have the opportunity to continue drawing and inventing at the Chateau of Cloux, near Amboise. A country manor house with grounds big enough to accommodate a flying machine," says DaVinci. "Along with ancillary buildings for The Uccellisa. And Mona Lisa."

"Impressive," says Lisa enthusiastically.

"You must be talking about me," says Giocondo who just walked in.

Giocondo struts over to DaVinci, stands behind him and begins his usual critique of the portrait in progress. "It's been five years and that's how far you've gotten, Maestro?"

"Six years but who's counting, Mr. Giocondo," DaVinci responds.

"I have an idea how to make the portrait even more original," says Giocondo. "Why not start over, considering you'll never finish at this turtle's pace."

"I have great respect for turtles, but my respect for you is on the wane," says DaVinci.

Lisa pipes up, "On the wane as well."

Giocondo, ignoring them both, continues to set up his idea.

He walks from DaVinci, past the easel and stands behind his wife. He positions himself directly in back of her right side and puts his right hand on her shoulder. "Maestro to Maestro, what do you think?" asks Giocondo.

DaVinci, expressionless, takes his arm out of the support, puts his paintbrush down and stands.

"I will get a blank codex and see what we shall see," DaVinci says, calmly. He leaves.

"If he never comes back, Francesco," says Lisa, "nobody would blame him."

"I would. And he'll come back. With a codex," says Giocondo with attitude.

"And a vengeance I hope," says Lisa with attitude.

Minutes pass. Then DaVinci comes back with a codex. A large codex. Again, he sits down at his usual place and starts sketching in earnest. "You can't move a muscle until I say you can," demands DaVinci. "No blinking. No twitching. No breathing."

Giocondo says, "Obviously, you think this is a good idea," says Giocondo.

"And no talking!" says DaVinci, his voice raised. "I do see an interesting composition, Mr. Giocondo,. But it could be any man standing in back of your lovely wife with his hand on her shoulder. It could be one of your Venetian competitors in the wool and silk industry. It could be an escaped prisoner. It could be the archbishop. It could be the devil himself."

"I have already solved that problem," says a defiant Giocondo. "I will have the round seal of the wool guild embroidered on my right sleeve. So my identity would be eminently clear."

"If you do not stop talking, Mr. Giocondo, I will take inspiration from Savonarola. And slash your precious portrait with my medieval sword," threatens DaVinci. "Then throw it on the fire."

"Vengeance is his," says Lisa, under her breath.

Giocondo walks toward DaVinci. He says, calmly, "Tomorrow, I am going to Rome. I will make time to visit the Sistine Chapel. With the pope. We will look up at the ceiling and be mesmerized by the genius selected by the pope—and the work that has been accomplished in such a brief period of time." Giocondo gets in DaVinci's face. "I will be sure to pass along your sincere compliments on the progress of another masterpiece by the great artist, Michelangelo Buonarrati.

THAT NIGHT, LISA AND FRANCESCO ARE HAVING A LATE supper in their dining room. Understated yet beautifully appointed, the dishes, flatware and glasses are the finest in all things culinary.

The couple sits across from each other in silence. In front of them are perfectly composed plates of tortellini covered in a sauce of thick, rich, green pesto.

They drink white wine from the Sangiovese region. There is fresh bread on the table in a handmade basket. It is white bread, a sign of Renaissance wealth and nobility. Go figure.

"I'm surprised you put meat in the tortellini," comments Giocondo, his mouth full.

"Mushrooms," Lisa responds, quietly.

"I know meat when I eat meat, Lisa." he argues.

"This is a special recipe developed by Leo's cook," she coldly replies. "I was lucky enough to get a private lesson on mixing the mushrooms with shallots, garlic and tomato paste to fill the pasta. And use only Genovese basil, pine nuts, olive oil and parmesan to make the pesto."

"Leo, Leo, Leo," taunts Giocondo. "Perhaps you should have married Leo."

"I am forever married to you, Francesco," says Lisa. "Unless you get a special dispensation in Rome."

Giocondo takes a huge sip of wine from his glass. Lisa takes a huge sip of wine from hers.

"I will be leaving for Rome tomorrow to advance one of the biggest and most important business opportunities for both the wool guild and the silk guild," he says, condescendingly.

"Will the she-wolves be advancing with you?" she asks, innocently.

Giocondo rips a piece of white bread and chews it like some starving, savage beast.

"What will they do while you discuss grounds for an annulment request with the pope?"

Lisa continues. "Grounds that include you, the petitioner, had never intended to be permanently married. Or faithful."

"No Italian husband intends to be unfaithful, Lisa," says Giocondo, seething. "It all depends on his wife."

"In the catholic church, the grounds for divorce are similar yet different," she explains.

"A man may request a divorce if his wife was unfaithful just once. However, if a woman requests a divorce, she has to prove that her husband was unfaithful. Every night. Or guilty of incest."

Giocondo pours more wine into his glass. "Since when are you so well-versed in the rules of annulment and divorce?" he asks.

"I seek all the experts around me," she answers.

"Nuns and monks have no expertise in that area," he says with sarcasm. "The pope himself? That is another story altogether."

"So you have discussed the possibilities before," says Lisa.

"Yes, Lisa," he admits, "I have."

"With the pope?" Lisa asks.

"With the pope who is the elevated, designated and consecrated expert in that area," says Giocondo, defensively. "Expert, judge and jury."

"Did you discuss petitioning for annulment or divorce on the grounds of adultery?" Lisa responds honestly.

"Yes, Lisa," he also responds honestly. "That subject has come up in conversation."

"Which means, Francesco Giocondo, I would be the petitioner," she says, definitively. "And you would be the betrayer."

"Well, LaGioconda, I could petition for either an annulment or a divorce on the grounds that you refuse to have children," calmly says Giocondo. "Or on the more damning grounds that you are a murderer."

"You don't want to go there, Frankie. It would not bode well," warns Lisa.

"Not bode well for you, Lisa. The church would grant my choice of either an annulment or a divorce," Giocondo continues, firmly. "On the spot."

Nearly another year has passed, and DaVinci is now more interested in making his inventions a reality than with finishing Mona Lisa's portrait. Truth be told, his career as a painter may be close to the end. He can still draw well with his left hand. His right hand? The ulnar nerve palsy has become so severe, it is difficult for DaVinci to hide the disability from himself, let alone others.

There are ruins of a military fortress on the grounds of the basilica. Far removed from the existing buildings that house the monks, the art and the ongoing religious services, the fortress has become DaVinci's workshop. An escape from the painful reality that is his life here and now.

Inside one of the last existing turrets, he has established a quasi construction site.

Since DaVinci can no longer accomplish the majority of work by himself, he has assembled an army of workmen, apprentices, students and would-be architects to explore and build the figments of his futuristic imagination.

One of the monks is leading Giocondo to DaVinci's workshop.

"What is this? It looks like the Roman ruins below The Palazzo Vecchio," says Giocondo.

"Big shot Giocondo doesn't know history," says the monk. "Not Roman. It is a military fortification left from the Wars in Lombardy. Between Milan and Florence, your home town."

The monk gestures for Giocondo to follow him.

THERE IS ORGANIZED CHAOS INSIDE THE CRUMBLING turret. Men of all shapes, sizes and talents swarm around each other like killer bees in a building frenzy...from hammering and sawing to soldering and sanding. Students are encouraged to draw on the walls and they do so with abandon.

DaVinci, on a ladder, sketches a huge version of Judas' elbow spilling the salt in The Last Supper.

Giocondo walks in and is surprised by all the wings and things. DaVinci sees him, then alerts the workers to stop working. DaVinci gestures for Giocondo to come closer, and announces:

"Most of you must know Francesco Giocondo. Because most of you have family and friends working in one of his powerful guilds, be it wool or be it silk."

The workers whistle and applaud. A smiling Giocondo modestly bows to them in response.

"Since Mr. Giocondo and I are about to have an extremely boring conversation," DaVinci says, there are now tables set up outside with delicious refreshments for you to enjoy. Manga!"

The workers scramble to the exit in search of fresh air and fresh food. DaVinci, still on the ladder, sits on one of the rungs, giving him the vantage point of talking down to Giocondo.

"This is some operation you have here," comments Giocondo. "Who's footing the bill?"

"My friend Nicolo rents this space for a hefty contribution," DaVinci explains. "As you well know, Servite monks don't compromise when it comes to funding the basilica. Let me show you what we've been up to. Oh, by the way. Young Machiavelli seems to be quite smitten with Lisa."

DaVinci, holding the ladder with his left hand for support, climbs down to give Giocondo a factory tour, one incredible scale model after another. Like a museum curator, he begins:

"This is my baby, the armored tank."

"This is a scythed chariot."

"A tread-wheel machine gun."

"A machine I designed with sixteen crossbows."

"The stone-hurling catapult. Feel free to lift one of the stones." Giocondo declines.

"My pride and joy? A flying machine designed to drop bombs and arrows on the enemy. All of this is why I invited you here today. To invest with Nicolo in manufacturing the future."

Giocondo is disgusted. "For a pacifist, you certainly are enamored with the armament. But you're not really a pacifist. You're a master manipulator with the art of covert manipulation."

DaVinci climbs back up on the ladder to continue his left-handed salt sketch.

Giocondo's rage rages. "You take Machiavelli's money on the premise of innovation, not annihilation. You charm the monks to feed you, house you and idolize you like a demigod.

Giocondo stands closer to the ladder and continues his rant. "Are all the men out there even getting paid? Anything? Or are they content to be in the presence of some legendary awesomeness? Are you the gifted DaVinci? Or the DaVinci who is skilled at taking all the gifts he can get?"

Giocondo looks up and yells at the top of his lungs, "And are you proud, Sir, of turning my own wife against me under the guise of mutual respect and friendship?!"

DaVinci looks down and quietly says, "No, Mr. Giocondo. You did that all by yourself."

DAYS LATER, LISA, WEARING A SIMPLE DRESS, IS IN THE studio packing. DaVinci, as always, sits on his cushioned wood stool in front of the easel. Miraculously, the Mona Lisa subject looks finished and fantastic. But the background is so far from being done, it could be the artwork's undoing.

Giocondo walks in like he always does. Well-heeled, confident and ready to rock. He carries a leather pouch nearly bursting with whatever is stuffed inside.

"How did you know I'd be here today, Francesco?" Lisa asks. "Read some tea leaves?"

"Our house reeks of sugar cakes, Giocondo says. "It nauseates me. As does tea."

"I find that herbal tea like chamomile can gently settle the stomach," comments DaVinci. "Especially when paired with Lisa's freshly-baked cakes."

Giocondo steps in front of DaVinci to closely examine the portrait. Sensing some impending bad mojo from her husband, Lisa walks over to become a participating referee.

Stumped, Giocondo asks, "Is that a bridge?"

"A symbolic bridge," answers DaVinci.

"A bridge between the beginning and the end," Lisa says.

"I will commission an artist to demolish that bridge, and paint a background that belongs behind my Mona Lisa," Giocondo says emphatically. "Because I am taking the portrait with me. Today. Rumor has it the King of France wants to treat you like a king with full relocation benefits. Like trading one of his chateaus for one of your portraits. This one. Not happening, monsieur."

"If you put your hands on this portrait, a very loud bell will be rung to immediately summon my security. Then, just as swiftly, the poliziotti will arrive to arrest you for stealing. And the verdict will be just as swift, along with some very bad press. Resulting in the demise of your status, your nobility and your global domination of silk and wool and auroserici," DaVinci says. "Capiche?"

"Tea leaves would have foretold you would respond this way," Giocondo says. "So I came prepared." He holds up the bulging leather pouch. "I, renown businessman that I am, contacted the Duke of Milan to learn the price he paid for The Lady with an Ermine. Or, as I prefer calling it,

The Bitch With A Badger. Or...hummm...The Beaver With A Beaver."

Lisa, very upset, says, "Don't do this, Francesco. I am begging you."

"Beg away, assassina, warns Giocondo. "You play no part in my negotiation."

Giocondo puts the pouch stuffed with cash on the table near the paint palette, saying, "Here is the exact amount paid by the Duke for his artwork. I have made a generous increase in that amount for all the drawings and the two canvases you managed to produce before the final product. I do not steal. I have never stolen anything. What would Mother Mary and her son think of me if I did?"

"As memory serves, Mr Giocondo," says DaVinci, "This is exactly what I said to you in the very beginning: My compensation is discussed only when I finish a project. Precisely when that project is finished is determined by me and only me."

"Well, I don't remember," says Giocondo. "So you take the cash and I take the painting."

Giocondo walks around the painting...waves his fingers above it...walks back to wave his fingers above the pouch... opens it...shows DaVinci the contents and sits across in the vacant chair.

"A classic buyer seller arrangement," Giocondo explains. "The money for the merch. Yes, DaVinci. Your art is my merchandise which I have waited years and years for and it is humiliating. I can tell by the grimace on your egotistical face that it is sinful to equate dirty money with pristine paintings. Yet, somehow, someone always pays up front, or offers a commission to become a patron of the arts. Take the revered and respected catholic church with their Bank of God. Paid holy bucks to Michelangelo for The Sistine Chapel ceiling. A much higher remuneration than yours for The Last Supper wall." (And lest we not forget DaVinci's Daddy Warbucks: Nicolo Machiavelli.)

"Perhaps, Mr. Giocondo," suggests DaVinci, "An angel will visit my studio tonight. So, in the morning, the background is finished and our buyer seller arrangement can be consummated at last."

"The same angel who finished the virgin's face in Bartolomeo's annunciaton," says Giocondo.

"Francesco. You know that story?" Lisa asks, surprised.

Giocondo says, "Every kid knows that story, Lisa. It's a fairy tale that's been turned around as a parental threat. My father used to warn me and my brothers: What do you expect, boys. An angel to come down at night and finish your morning chores. Or your homework. Or your vegetables."

"Did you finish?" asks DaVinci.

"Of course we finished. We always finish. Which is more than I can say for you, DaVinci," Giocondo fires back. "Another artist will finish and alter the background to my liking,"

"And what might that be?" DaVinci responds as politely as possible.

Giocondo politely responds, "I want to see it painted,

painted, painted, painted black.

DaVinci stands up and takes a strong stance directly in front of the painting. He lifts his left arm parallel to his body in defiance.

"Since your right hand is shot, I'd be doing you a favor," says Giocondo.

In response, with superhuman effort, DaVinci lifts his right arm. Even as Giocondo advances towards him with menace, the artist trembles - but holds steady. Behold...Vitruvian man.

"I would rather die than have this portrait taken from me, unfinished," says DaVinci with conviction. "So let these be the words carved on my headstone, "I have offended God and mankind because my work did not reach the quality it should have."

"I suggest something a tad shorter," Giocondo remarks. "Here lies a bullshit artist."

"Lisa. Get the bell," DaVinci demands. Lisa hesitates. She looks at her husband. She looks at DaVinci. She slowly walks toward DaVinci and reaches underneath the cushioned wooden stool.

With tears streaming down her face, Lisa unlocks a mechanism and removes a large bell that has been hidden in case of emergency. She holds the bell above her head like the statue of liberty.

"Ring the bell, Lisa," DaVinci commands. "Long and loud."

Giocondo stands up and plaintively stares at his wife. He stares at DaVinci still guarding the portrait. He suddenly has a very real epiphany that appears to be an expression of grief.

"Maestro," Giocondo asks quietly. "Would you be kind enough to grant me a final look?"

DaVinci slowly lowers both arms and steps aside; Lisa slowly lowers the bell. Giocondo stares at the artwork, puts his hand on his chest and takes a deep breath.

Without a word, he begins to walk out. But some realization makes him turn and walk back in. Lisa and DaVinci become more and more tense as Giocondo gets closer and closer to the portrait.

He takes the pouch full of money, turns around and leaves the studio. Forever.

HOURS LATER, LISA AND DAVINCI ARE SITTING ON A BENCH in a lush garden wild with natural beauty.

Birds sing in trees. Small animals happily bound about. Look! There's a kitten. There's its mother.

"Where has your carriage brought us this fine day," asks Lisa.

"Sarcasm is not a flattering quality, my dear," DaVinci says. "My response to where is here we sit in the Secret Garden of the Medici.

"Is there anything the Medici family doesn't have?" Lisa comments.

"Peace," he says. "Second response to you is truth without sarcasm. This day has been far from fine. Unfortunate. Unbearable. And you, Lisa, must consult a physician or a priest or a psychic to discover why your husband has been spiraling down and further down. It is a critical situation."

A lone peacock struts back and forth through the garden. It walks in front of Lisa and DaVinci, displays his feathers, then continues down a long, rhododendron path before strutting out of sight.

"One of the medical students at the Ospedale degli

Innocenti gave me a studied diagnosis," Lisa reveals. "A one-word diagnosis, actually."

"What word?" asks DaVinci.

"Trauma," answers Lisa.

"There is no result in nature without a cause. Understand the cause and you will have no need of the experiment," he explains.

"Sometimes, Leo," she says, "I have no idea what you mean."

"Sometimes, I have no idea what I mean either," he says, smiling.

Lisa says, "The medical student said that trauma can be physical or mental. Even emotional."

"Those students are truly ahead of their teachers," he says. "Trauma is from the Greek word meaning wound."

"Francesco looks as handsome as ever," she says. "I see no wound."

"His wound may not be an exterior one, Lisa," he says, softly. "Which can make the trauma much more difficult to determine and often impossible to treat."

"You have studied side-by-side with the doctors and students at the hospital," says Lisa. "Please, Leo. Please tell me how to help my husband."

"I have gained much medical knowledge," he says. "More about the body than the brain.

I am so sorry, my dear. I do not know the answer to that question. What I do know is you,

Mona Lisa, may find the answer well before any one of us."

"He wanted to divorce me. At least get our marriage annulled," Lisa says.

"When in Rome," DaVinci responds.

"He did neither. I wanted to leave him so many times. Run away. Go back to the farm. Or stay close and live in the basement surrounded by The Uccellisa," she admits. " I did neither."

Lisa confesses, "I am not afraid to be alone. I am afraid to leave Francesco alone."

DaVinci stands up and says to Lisa, "I will be right back."

"Where are you going, Leo?" she asks.

"I will be right back with nourishment for the soul in your hour of need," he says.

He leaves. Lisa sits there alone to think about trauma - her husband's and possibly her own.

The mother cat comes over to Lisa and lays at her feet.

"Hello, beauty," Lisa says to the cat, "I would love to take you home with me. But Francesco, he is my husband, forbids your sharp claws anywhere near his beloved upholstery fabrics."

Four kittens with the same markings come over and lay by the cat. "Please watch over your children, Mamma." Lisa says to the cat. "Never take your eyes off them. Even for a second."

Lisa picks up one of the kittens, snuggles with it, and slowly puts it back with the cat.

DaVinci, true to his word, returns after just a few minutes. He carries a small tray which he puts on the bench next to Lisa. She sees an unfamiliar confection in two silver bowls. The cat is curious but stretches and walks away down the rhododendron path. Her four fur babies follow.

DaVinci puts a silver spoon into one of the bowls and hands it to Lisa. He puts a silver spoon into the other bowl for himself. They lift their spoons and dig into something cold and unique.

"Mother of God, this is amazing," exclaims Lisa.

"I agree. A secret recipe in the secret garden." DaVinci says. "Cosimo Ruggieri, an alchemist on the Medici payroll, invented it. The family vehemently demands exotic fruit sorbet after every meal. So Mr. Ruggieri picked up the frozen gauntlet and made more heaven in a bowl. From fresh cream with bergamot, lemons and oranges.

Lisa, her mouth full, points at the frozen delight and asks, "Does it have a name?"

Nodding his head DaVinci happily says, "Gelato."

"If that family had to make a choice, I wonder," says Lisa. "Would it be gelato - or peace."

"A toss up," says DaVinci.

As they continue eating, Lisa asks, amazed, "They have their own alchemist?"

LATE AFTERNOON THAT SAME DAY, LISA WALKS DOWN a lush, floral-planted path to her palatial Medici-adjacent home. She appears drained, sad and spent.

Lisa unlocks the magnificent front door and enters the foyer with its extravagant moldings and empty walls. She walks into the living room and sees Giocondo sitting on one of the elegant silk sofas. The portraits of his ancestors that were hanging on the wall are now on the floor below.

"Francesco," Lisa asks softly. "Why are all your family portraits on the floor?"

"I don't want them looking at me," he says in a monotone. "Ashamed."

Giocondo stands up, walks to the portraits and turns them around, one by one, to face the wall. This takes him some time, because the portraits, in their gold frames, are heavy and hard to move. He walks back to the sofa and sits back where he was. A side table with flowers is near by.

Lisa walks over and sits by her husband. He moves away. She moves closer. He stays put.

"Where did you go after the studio," Lisa asks. "Did you take a walk to clear your head?"

"I walked back to my office at the silk guild. Then I walked to my office at the wool guild," Giocodo says, "Nothing clears my head, Lisa."

"Did you go back for some important guild business?" Lisa wonders.

"Yes and no. I went back to make an announcement," Gicondo explains. "I gathered as many of my senior guild associates as possible to tell them I would be taking a leave of absence."

Lisa, dumfounded, shakes her head in disbelief and grabs her husband's hand. Immediately, he pulls his hand away from hers. He starts to cough, then harder, then has trouble breathing.

Lisa runs to the kitchen and pours a glass of apple juice.

She runs back to the living room and gives the glass of juice to Francesco. He takes a few sips, then a few more and gives the glass back to Lisa. She puts it the side table.

HOURS EARLIER, IN AN AUDITORIUM, GIOCONDO IS READY to address a large crowd filled with his most loyal and talented guild managers. His outfit is understated, without that flashy blue consul sash.

Ami and Nomi stand like celebrities in the front row. DeLuca, modest, is standing there, too.

Giocondo announces, "All the travel back and forth to Rome, along with the pressure of getting the deal done, has adversely affected my health. I need a break to rest and recuperate, be it a week or a month."

There is a highly audible gasp from the assembled crowd.

"I have complete confidence in your management acumen, especially that of Mr. Deluca," Giocondo says.

DeLuca turns around and reluctantly waves. There is big applause for him from the crowd.

"But, as your Consul," Giocodo continues, "I am making a few decisions before I leave.

First, my assistants, Ami and Nomi, are being promoted to oversee our operations in Milan."

The twins turn around and start blowing kisses like the movie stars they think they are.

Except for a couple of coughs and the sound of one hand clapping, the crowd is silent.

"They will be working directly under the Duke's personal supervision," Giocondo adds.

"Next, I am amending my current rules regarding all guild members and their volunteer work on the Uccellisa. From this day forward, anyone who volunteers will receive a time-and-a-half payment for their charitable hours spent. If they work on Saturday, that pay will double. On Sunday, the pay for volunteering to make more children happy will be tripled."

Cheers and whistles from the assembled multitude.

"Be well, my steadfast friends," Giocondo says with emotion, "And I will try to do the same." Rousing applause for him fills the entire space.

BACK IN THEIR LIVING ROOM, LISA IS DRINKING THE APPLE juice.

"That was heroic, Frankie," Lisa says. "That was brave".

In a near a whisper, Giocondo asks, "Why weren't you brave enough to ring the bell, Lisa?"

"I couldn't," she says. "Not for Leo. Not for anyone."

"You should have rung the bell six times," he states emphatically.

Lisa, confused, says, "The church rings the bell six times, Francesco. For a funeral."

"Precisamente," Giocondo answers.

"I am making you something to eat. And you will eat it all," she demands.

Lisa again runs to the kitchen, grabs some linen napkins, and opens a storage cabinet to retrieve a wooden tray. She starts preparing food like a frenzied line cook.

Lisa slices a cantaloupe into an ornamental metal bowl.

She places thin pieces of prosciutto onto a decorative mosaic plate.

She chooses a variety of cheeses to accompany generous servings of that noble white bread.

When everything is on the tray, Lisa rushes back into the living room. Giocondo is gone. She puts the tray down and starts looking for him in a panic.

She runs into the dining room.

She runs back into the kitchen.

She runs to the foyer by the magnificent front door. Here, Giocondo sits on the floor. Unmoving, like a statue, he stares at the big blank wall.

Lisa, relieved but winded, runs back into the living room and retrieves the tray.

Lisa returns to the foyer and puts the tray down next to her husband. Then, she sits on the floor beside him and takes a deep, cleansing breath.

"Remember the picnics we used to have, Frankie?" Lisa asks lovingly. "This is another picnic. But better because we never had cantaloupe before."

"I remember. You were pregnant," he says.

Lisa eats a piece of prosciutto, and chews it with delighted gourmet appreciation.

"You just ate a piece of ham, Lisa," comments Giocondo.

"I forgot how good good prosciutto can be," Lisa says.

Giocondo eats a long piece of prosciutto. Then he eats a piece or two of cheese. Then a bite of cantaloupe. Then, he can't resist taking a thick piece of bread and covering it with a pile of more prosciutto and another type of cheese.

Lisa eats some cheese, followed by some cantaloupe, followed by another piece of prosciutto.

"Do you go on picnics with Machiavelli? Giocondo asks.

"What kind of question is that, Francesco?" Lisa wonders. "I never met him, let alone have a picnic with him. Where did that fiction come from?"

"DaVinci said Machiavelli was smitten with you," Giocondo explains.

"Maybe he saw me in the workshop, where all my sanding and soldering took his breath away," Lisa responds. "Maybe Leo was just trying to stir things up."

"Sanding and soldering what?" Giocondo asks.

"Wings," Lisa says. "With feathers, without feathers, in wood, in metal, I don't really care."

The two of them eat most of what was on the tray. They both seem a little more relaxed. Until Giocondo again starts staring, unblinking, at the empty foyer wall.

"Do you see that, Lisa? Giocondo asks. "Right there," he says, pointing to a particular place.

"I don't see anything, Francesco," Lisa says. "Nothing. Except an empty wall."

"I will never see my Mona Lisa portrait hanging there. I will never see my Mona Lisa again," he says, nearly in tears. "A realization that struck me like a thunderbolt in the studio today. It was the same thunderbolt that shook my entire body and soul when my baby died," he whispers.

"She was my baby, too," she says.

"If you kill someone, you can no longer claim them as your own," he says.

"Trauma," Lisa says.

"That is a word the pope used," Giocondo explains, surprised. "Greek for wound."

"You talked to the pope about Francesca?" she says, angry. "Who gives you the right."

Lisa stands up, takes the tray and walks back into the kitchen.

She starts cleaning the tray and tossing the leftovers.

Giocondo comes in and opens the door to the liquor cabinet.

Lisa immediately closes it.

"I thought your plan was to consult the pope about the annulment process," says Lisa. "Or the divorce process, or the putting-me-on-trial-for-murder process, whichever was faster. That is the main reason you went to Rome, yes?"

Giocondo confesses, "No. That wasn't me bringing up the possibility of annulment or divorce or prison. It was Altro."

"Altro," says Lisa, confused. "Who or what is Altro?"

"I had to give a name to what was happening," he says

honestly. "I believe it helps me cope."

"In my vocabulary, Altro means other, Francesco," she says.

GIOCONDO PACES BACK AND FORTH AND EXPLAINS, "HE is the other Francesco. It is Altro who says and does the terrible things I would never say or do. The voice is mine. The body is mine. But it is Altro who is out of control. Out of character. Out of reality. Out of his mind.

Across Europe and beyond, I continue to dominate the thriving fabric industry," Giocondo says. "While Altro is the one unraveling."

Lisa, holding the metal bowl, drops it. Some cantaloupe and its sticky juices spill on the floor.

Oblivious, Giocondo continues, "I design a robe for DaVinci one day - Altro calls him a bullshit artist the next. I proudly support your Uccellisa effort - Altro chastises the guild members for their participation."

Lisa, shaking her head, picks up the slippery pieces of cantaloupe and puts them back in the bowl. She can't believe what her husband is saying.

"Altro held the paintbrush and stained the DaVinci canvas purple," he explains.

Lisa finds a large towel and gets on her knees to wipe the floor.

"I would laugh at any relationship between LaGioconda and a fanatico like Machievelli," declares Giocondo. "It would've been ridiculous to me. But not to Altro. He was jealous."

Lisa is still wiping the floor.

"When did Altro come into your head, Francesco?" Lisa asks respectfully.

"I think," Giocondo guesses, "Altro showed up when Maestro declined to paint my portrait because I could not sit still."

"Your portrait?" Lisa says, incredulous.

"Yes, Lisa," Giocondo informs his wife, "At first, I asked him to paint me. Whatever the price, I would pay it. I wanted an original DaVinci more than anything I ever wanted in my life.

"Anything?" Lisa asks.

"No. I wanted Francesca back in her crib sound asleep." Giocondo takes a deep breath and continues. "That is when Altro appeared and lied to you on my behalf."

"How convenient," "Lisa remarks. "Altro lied to me, your wife, for you, my husband."

"Altro promised that DaVinci would include drawings of Francesca if you would sit and be his Mona Lisa, whatever the price." Giocondo explains. "Of course, Maestro definitely had his own ulterior motives. But he didn't have Altro. I did."

Lisa stands up and throws the wet cloth at him.

She takes a bottle from the liquor cabinet and some short-stem glasses from another.

"Would Altro care for a little grappa?" Lisa teases.

"This is serious, Lisa," Giocondo says, obviously hurt.

Lisa fills two glasses with a generous pour of the great Italian spirit. One for her, one for him.

"I know that, Francesco," says Lisa. "I am proud of your admitting that the condition is serious and escalating by the day. It takes a self-aware and confident man to actually say it. Out loud."

Lisa holds out her glass and gives him a look.

Reluctantly, Francesco holds out his glass.

They give a classic clink and drink the grappa in one shot.

Francesco holds out his empty glass and indicates to Lisa he wants a refill.

She shakes her head, then puts the two empty glasses on the counter.

"I wasn't lashing out at you before I left for Rome," Giocondo admits. "Lashing out is not the Giocondo style. That was Altro."

"Ah, that was Altro," Lisa says.

"And I never talked to the pope about dissolving our marriage," says Giocondo. "I talked with him privately about my anguish of losing baby girl."

"What was his response? Something like: Let the little children come to me and do not hinder them, for to such belongs the kingdom of heaven." Lisa asks with anger. "That is why the pope is the pope, Lisa continues. "Always ready, willing and able to comfort a suffering parishioner with the perfect quote from Jesus. You see, Francesco, my father also made his children read the bible. Religiously," she says. "The testaments. Old and new."

Giocondo is taken aback by Lisa's intense reaction.

"I also talked to someone for a scientific approach to trauma. Someone who works with doctors every day, Lisa says. "DaVinci told me that there is no result in nature without a cause. Understand the cause and you will have no need of the experiment."

"You spoke to DaVinci about my problem?" says an offended Giocondo.

"DaVinci was an eye witness, Francesco," she reminds him. "Besides, you spoke to the pope."

"What does no need of the experiment mean," he asks her.

"I didn't understand it, either, Frankie," she admits. "But when you introduced Altro, it all became crystal clear."

"Lisa, I am incapable of making anything crystal clear," says Giocondo.

She explains, "Altro is the experiment you use to hide a guilty conscience that was probably caused by the trauma in the first place."

"Really? Between you, me and Altro," he states, "You're the guilty one in this conversation."

"What else did the pope have to say?" Lisa asks.

"That the trauma inside me is the devil. And heaven's cure is not only about getting justice," Giocondo tells Lisa, "It's about forgiving ourselves as much as we do others."

"In that case, I also have an Altro. A double burden. One Lisa to carry her own pain of loss. The other Lisa who vowed to always carry yours," she says. "And you don't even know why,"

"My baby died," Francesco fires back. "That is why, assassina."

"Is Altro calling me that?" she asks.

"No." he says with conviction. "I am."

Lisa washes the tray, then the glasses.

"Why is different from how," she says.

"I don't know what you're talking about, Lisa," Giocondo says.

She dries the tray.

She dries the glasses.

She puts the top on the grappa bottle.

"Come upstairs," Lisa says, quietly. "Leave Altro behind."

Lisa puts the tray, glasses and bottle back in their assigned cabinets. She leaves the doors open.

"I will tell you why and how, Frankie," she says. "I hope to god...

Lisa closes one cabinet door.

...his son...

Lisa closes another cabinet door

...and his son's mother...

Lisa closes another cabinet door.

...will give me the strength to do it."

THEY ARE IN THEIR PALATIAL MASTER BEDROOM. LISA SITS on her twin bed, Giocondo sits on his.

Lisa takes off her shoes and walks toward the glass balcony doors. On the way, she passes a closed armoire with the Mona Lisa dress hanging on the front.

She opens the glass doors to let in the breeze and the fading light of a Florentine sunset.

Lisa asks: "Do you want me to take your shoes off, Francesco?"

He answers: "Better keep them on. In case I have to run out of here, screaming."

Lisa walks back toward the beds, and goes to the large bureau between the two. She opens one of the top drawers and takes out something small and carefully wrapped.

She walks to Francesco, sits on his bed, unwraps the package and shows it to him. It is the uccello Lisa took from the trunk she had brought for the nuns at the Ospedale degli Innocenti.

Refusing to look at the little bird, Francesco turns his head away.

"Francesca loved my handmade birds that dangled from the ceiling on colorful ribbons," Lisa says. "I let all of them go to the nuns at the Ospedale degli Innocenti. Except this one. You know about that hospital, don't you Frankie. It is a foundling hospital. A baby hospital. The doctors there are specialists. They are experts on newborns, infants and toddlers. It took all my strength to speak with them weeks after our baby died."

Without looking at Lisa, Giocondo stands, walks to a chaise across the room and sits.

"My baby. She was mine," he says.

Lisa explains. "The doctors told me that one in four infants die before their first birthday."

"I wonder how many are murdered by their own mother," he fires back.

"The doctors told me there are many causes of infant mortality, " says Lisa. "Birth defects, disease, hunger, neglect,"

Giocondo cuts her off. "You are the poster mother for neglect, aren't you Lisa."

Lisa ignores his accusatory comment and continues. "But the leading cause of their mortality is something the medical community calls overlying."

"I don't care about the medical community and their so-called expertise, Lisa," he says. "You killed Francesca."

"How did I kill Francesca?" Lisa asks. "You never told me."

"More ways than I can count, assassina," Giocondo says. "Your milk was bad and it poisoned her. You took her outside in the carriage when it was raining and she caught a chill. You kept her in the sun too long and she died of fever. You never dressed her properly so she was exposed to a swarm of stinging insects. She ate dirt in the garden when you turned away, even for a second."

"Overlying is the leading cause, Francesco," Lisa says. It is normal for parents to roll over when they sleep. If they take their baby to bed with them, or move a pillow, or toss a blanket, it's called overlying. Because the baby is trapped underneath. That is how these babies die, Francesco. The why? The baby cannot breathe and the poor thing smothers to death."

"I never had Francesca in the bed with me. Not even for a nap," Giocondo says in defense.

"Neither did I," Lisa says in defense. "I replayed everything in my mind about that night, over and over. Thousands of times. And then I remembered what I saw that morning. Do you remember the night before she died in her crib?"

"I tried thousands of times to forget. I still do. And I will leave this house forever if you try to make me remember," Giocondo vows.

Lisa goes back to the bureau and opens a larger drawer at the bottom. She takes out a lovely silk baby blanket and brings it over to her husband. He looks at the blanket. Then looks in horror.

"The silk guild lovingly made this baby blanket for us." Lisa says, softly. "With a tiny, hand- embroidered bird and the initials F.M.G. Francesca Maria Giocondo."

Giocondo shakes his head, stands up and walks to the glass doors.

Without looking at Lisa, he says, "I came home from work late that night. You were sound asleep. So I was very, very quiet. I always kissed Francesca good night, no matter what."

"I think—no, yes—I remember going into her room. Her pretty pink room," he continues. "Francesca seemed to me a little fussier than usual."

Giocondo starts closing the balcony doors.

"I saw her little cheeks were red," he says. "I thought my baby was cold."

He struggles with the doors as if they were made of lead, and continues to tell what happened:

"So I took the blanket from the back of your rocking chair," Giocondo says in a whisper. "Then I covered my precious child and gave her a gentle kiss on the forehead."

"I nursed Francesca in that chair," Lisa explains. "I put that blanket on the back of that chair to admire it every day and night. I would never put that blanket in her crib because it was so delicate, the silk could never be cleaned if she put it in her tiny mouth or even touched it."

With the same body language as the exhausted Bartolomeo three centuries before, Giocondo can barely make the journey across the room to his twin bed.

Completely distraught, Giocondo lies on the bed and curls up in a fetal position. Lisa goes to her husband, sits on the bed and holds him as he begins to cry and cry. Like a baby.

"It was an accident," soothes Lisa. "The worse accident any parent can imagine."

Giocondo, through his tears, says, "You knew. You knew all this time that it was my fault our baby died. And you let me say assassina and murderer and killer. Why didn't you tell me? Why didn't you punish me? Oh my god, Lisa. I wouldn't even go to Francesca's burial because I knew you would be standing there, weeping with your family. And my family. And DeLuca, her beloved godfather, who always made our baby laugh."

A sudden softness of clear moonlight washes over them as Lisa whispers to her husband,

"It's not too late, Frankie."

GIOCONDO AND LAGIOCONDA WOULD SPEND MOST OF THE next month on a magical mystery tour of forgiveness. They would encourage each other through a compassionate recovery. Embolden each other to restore and resurrect the marriage. Explore each other in the therapeutic mercy of sexual healing. And share bowl-after-bowl of hot chick-pea soup with thick white bread.

The month begins at the Cimitero Monumentale, the hilltop cemetery on the south bank of the Arno River, east of the center of Florence with a spectacular view. Lisa chose this location because here, little egrets build their nests on poplar trees where no harm can come to their hatchlings.

Hand-in-hand, Lisa leads Giocondo to a section where headstones are smaller than the taller, more ornate stones that surround them. She carries a bouquet of baby's breath. They stop at one particular headstone. The marble has been simply yet beautifully carved with the initials F.M.G. next to a pretty baby bird. Lisa puts the bouquet next to the stone. The parents stand there and begin to say a familiar prayer, out loud. Suddenly, every other person in the cemetery joins them:

"May holy Mary, the angels, and all the saints above watch over this bambina. Yes, she has gone forth from this life, but be pacified that your baby is forever blessed in heaven. Amen."

Leaving the cemetery, Lisa passes a statue of the Virgin Mary and touches her hand, just like she did in the garden with DaVinci outside his basilica office/library.

AFTER A FEW PEACEFUL DAYS AT HOME, THEY ARE TAKEN by carriage to one of the sixteen country estates owned by the Medici and recently gifted to the Giocondo family for their contribution to the Florentine economy. Here, husband and wife write copious letters. She to the nuns at the Ospedale degli Innocenti...he to the monks and his guild managers. These letters contain instructions for an event Lisa and Francesco are planning after their return. The letters are sealed with a wax "G" and delivered by private (and pricey) couriers travelling on foot, on horseback or by boat.

But after weeks of living in such a quiet, remote and overly opulent environment, Lisa longs for something more her style. Since Giocondo will now do anything and everything to make his wife happy, they go from a wealth of oriental rugs to a natural wealth of cliff-side ruggedness.

WELCOME TO CINQUE TERRE ON THE ITALIAN RIVIERA.

Five villages built into sheer rock of a mountain overlooking the Mediterranean Sea. The ancient Romans were first, of course, to occupy this zone as a mighty, strategic stronghold. Luckily, they were brilliant engineers who invented concrete with a mixture of broken stones, lime, sand, and water. They discovered that supplementing the sand with a volcanic ash would produce an even harder material known as hydraulic mortar. Which was helpful when the challenge was a vertical build 812 meters high, (2,664 feet) over half a mile up.

Here, in a cozy but beautiful home with terraces that defy gravity, the working-on-being-happy couple would spend a week gazing down at an even more beautiful harbor. They also loved the four poster bed that the Giocondo's couldn't imagine how it could possibly be hoisted up the cliff.

Dante Alighieri may have compared the Cinque Terre with the rugged cliff of Purgatory in the Divine Comedy. But Lisa Giocondo compares it with the rugged cliffs of paradise on high.

Score one for Francesco.

They hike the Sentiero Azzuro (Azure Trail) connecting the five distinct and unique villages.

They gingerly walk the pebbled beach at Monterossa al Mare and together float on the sea.

They dine at every cucina and hole-in-the-wall, enjoying the local catch from anchovies, hake and mussels to squid, shrimp and octopus. The owners of these eateries all comment on how happy the couple seems—like newlyweds on their honeymoon—and pour them complimentary glasses of wine from vineyards planted on Cinque Terre's own perilously steep slopes.

There are many phrases in the dictionary to describe the word 'honeymoon'. But if a particular definition is 'a period of unusual harmony following the establishment of a new relationship', these two are certainly on one. And then some.

MUST ALL GOOD THINGS COME TO AN END? HOPEFULLY, NOT for Giocondo and LaGioconda.

They spend the last week of their month-long forgiveness journey giving themselves a dose of reality. And giving their Medici-adjacent home a major refresh and renewal.

Most of the rooms are being painted a bright white with

touches of sea blue.

Living room furniture is rearranged to make the space more conducive to company.

In the master bedroom, the large bureau is moved into another bedroom, along with the twin beds that, Lisa hopes, will help their future children sleep soundly. All to make room in the master for a four-poster bed just like the one in Cinque Terre, without the cliff-side hassle.

Most of that week is all the time they spend together in the garden. Giocondo dislikes digging, planting and replanting as much as he dislikes hiking. But he stays outside with Lisa sweating like the buff, sun-kissed gardener he has become.

Together, they plant many flowers and fruit trees that will bear lemons and cherries under their care. They plant a fig tree in Francesca's honor, to watch it grow tall and strong and sweet.

A flurry of notes and messages are couriered back and forth from their home to the monks, the nuns and Giocondo's point people at both guilds as plans for the upcoming event grows closer and closer by the day.

THE TIME HAS COME TO CELEBRATE DAVINCI DAY, which the city of Florence has declared a new and legal holiday sponsored by the Giocondo family. Come on, kids, let's get down and partay!

There, on the basilica grounds in front of the fortress that was DaVinci's workshop, a carnival atmosphere is in full swing. Along with families from peasantry to nobility, the nuns and monks are enjoying themselves like typical, fun-loving Italians.

There is a plethora of food to be had. Sweet and salty, hot and cold…whatever you like…all there for the scarfing down…all for free.

There is singing and dancing of popular songs by performed by masked merrymakers.

There are games to be played that are still being played today. Tag, hide-and -seek, horseshoe throwing, ring tossing, stilt walking and see sawing.

Pyrotechnics? Si, per favore. Including girandoles or whirling decorated wheels packed with fireworks suspended from a rope that's been hung high across the entire outdoor expanse.

And no DaVinci Day planner worth his un-spilled salt would forget Florence's passion of flag-waving. So every kid gets a mini version of il Tricolore, with the Uccellisa flying right on top.

But first, a word from our sponsor.

Giocondo walks to the podium to cheers and applause. He looks like a different man. Tan, relaxed, smiling, and cucumber-cool in a linen ensemble perfectly fit for California dreaming.

"Welcome to the first annual DaVinci Day in Florence," Giocondo announces. "As many of you know, Maestro DaVinci has packed up his toys and gone to France. With my painting."

The audience boos and jeers.

"But," Giocondo remarks, "I am sure he will miss Italy so much, Maestro will come home to us soon. With my painting. Meanwhile, we will take his spacious workshop and make it our own."

Giocondo points to the ruins of that military fortress that no longer looks quite as ruined.

New windows have been installed, and a whole second story has miraculously been built.

"DaVinci created scale models of his brilliant inventions in there," Giocondo explains.

"Most of those scale models have been crated and moved to Milan. Because the Milanese have funded a museum in his honor," Giocondo says. "But they didn't fund the first DaVinci Day,"

Again, the crowd whistles and applauds to communicate their excitement.

"Of course," Giocondo continues, "We did a little fundraising of our own. The Servite monks raised enough money to preserve thousands and thousands of his leather notebooks in a secure, undisclosed location. Safe. In perpetuity. With a forever supplement from the Giocondo family."

All the Servite monks from the basilica wave at the crowd to thundering applause.

"The nuns from the hospital," he continues, "will use charitable donations from the Uccellisa to move production from the basement to the refurbished space inside Maestro's former workshop."

All the nuns from the Ospedale degli Innocenti wave at the crowd to thundering applause.

"The first floor is dedicated to hand-making birds that dangle from the ceiling on colorful ribbons," Giocondo says. "The second floor is set up to track all orders that keep flying in."

"What about the empty basement?" continues Giocondo. "The nuns have decided to create a special research library for the doctors and medical students. To help our babies and infants thrive.

Finally, I would like to thank every member of the silk guild and the wool guild for putting such time and effort into their work and this community," he says. "And for putting up with me."

DeLuca nods. Giocondo starts to walk away from the podium, then stops and walks back.

"DaVinci produced over 35,000 words and 500 sketches about flying machines, the nature of air and bird flight. Especially his ornithopters with flapping wings. To demonstrate, here is the one person to whom all of us owe a debt we can never repay," says Giocondo. "But we can try."

As the workshop doors open, a very long platform is wheeled out by the men who worked with DaVinci inside. Standing on the platform is a woman wearing a leather tunic, tights and high boots.

It is Lisa. With wings.

So many, many years later, a man walks the long, paved path of an estate built like a palace. He continues toward the Château of Cloux, a country manor house in France's Loire Valley.

This is a man whose poise and posture indicates not only a pedigree of family wealth, but great economic strength and political influence. With the air of success and a wardrobe of subtlety, this is a man who doesn't need to strut, pose or flaunt himself like a peacock.

It's very good to be Francesco Giocondo.

He gets to the imposing front door and knocks. No answer. He knocks harder. Finally, a much older man opens the door to greet him.

It is Leonardo DaVinci. The same coiffed, cascading hair and beard. But now, his hair and his beard have turned white. He wears the twelve-color robe with magenta sleeves, literally hanging on his emaciated frame like a shroud over a skeleton.

"Welcome to France, Mr. Giocondo," says DaVinci.

With a tease, Giocondo replies, "I was in the neighborhood, so I decided to drop by."

"Lisa had written me that you were travelling to France for many reasons. Come," DaVinci suggests, "Let us sit in my gazebo and catch up on all things Giocondo."

The men walk slowly to a magnificent outdoor terrace overlooking acres of manicured grounds. There is a glass enclosure ready to be enjoyed, rain, shine or foreign invasion.

There are two bistro chairs and a table set with Limoges plates and cups, sugar, cream and a tray of macarons in many pastel colors. Giocondo drapes his long coat with multiple pockets over one of the chairs.

The two men sit at the table. DaVinci points to a mysterious cylindrical pot with a plunger and built-in filter screen.

"Coffee?" DaVinci asks Giocondo, who nods enthusiastically.

"I push the plunger down with my left hand, to slowly and steadily press the hot water through perfectly fresh, ground coffee. Et voila."

Again only using his left hand, DaVinci fills two cups. They both sip the steaming coffee with obvious satisfaction.

"Did you design this wonderful machine?" Giocondo asks.

"Of course," DaVinci says. "I call it the French Press. I told Lisa about the invention in one of my letters."

"You two must have written hundreds of letters to each other over these many years," says Giocondo. "I have no idea how Lisa reads your handwriting. No, that's not really true.

I saw her holding the letters up to a mirror. Because you

must be writing it all backwards."

"Your wife is not only an acute problem solver. But an excellent writer; accurate and extremely detail oriented," says DaVinci.

"Lisa wanted to see you. Here with me in person." Giocondo says. "But she is due to give birth in just a few weeks."

DaVinci asks, "What do your other children think of their new sibling-to-be?"

"They talk to Lisa's belly all the time," explains Gioicondo.

"Renzo, our older boy, talks about silk and wool like a Giocondo expert. He loves coming to work with me. And to see DeLuca, their godfather. Who knows why they find their LucaLuca surprisingly funny and entertaining.

Rocco, our younger boy, has a heart as big as his mother's. When DeLuca suddenly passed away, we dreaded telling our sons the sad news. Renzo took it like a man. Rocco took it like Rocco. He put his little hand on Lisa's shoulder and said: Don't worry, Mamma. LucaLuca is making our sister Francesca laugh up in heaven."

"How old is Rocco," DaVinci asks.

"He is five. Renzo is seven," Giocondo answers. "Both far wise beyond their years."

"Do they want a baby brother or sister?" DaVinci wonders.

Giocondo says, "We all just want a healthy baby and a healthy mamma."

"Will you allow your sons to choose the baby's name?" DaVinci wonders again.

"They named their cats Zetto and Calzone. So, no," Giocondo says. "Lisa and I have already chosen names. Lea for a girl. Leo for a boy."

DaVinci, hiding his emotion, eats a macaron and pours more coffee in both cups.

"One reason I came to France is on wedding business," says Giocondo. "A young count from the House of La Rochefoucauld will marry a woman he's never met. The Duke of Lorraine will celebrate the third marriage of his brother who is only a baron. But the holy roman emperor will be officiating, none the less. All have ordered fabric for the bride, groom, wedding party, after party, royal after party, morning after party, the list goes on. And on.

"And the couturiers who consider themselves artistes have the last word," says DaVinci

"Speaking of artistes," adds Giocondo. "Did you ever finish that unfinished background?"

"I added some mountains behind the bridge," says DaVinci. "And a winding road to the sea in the distance."

"I want to see the painting." Giocondo says. "That is another reason I travelled to France."

"It is locked in one of the royal vaults, Mr. Giocondo. Along with the crown jewels and priceless bottles of cognac," DaVinci says. "He was born in the Cognac region."

"Who was?" Giocondo wonders.

"My loyal friend Francis," DaVinci answers. "The King who owns the Mona Lisa."

"Your royal friend probably locked it up," Giocondo comments, "So you wouldn't keep changing the background or the foreground or remove the veil that covers her hair."

"I sold the Mona Lisa to his majesty. He was so obsessed with the portrait, he had to possess it, hide it and keep it for his eyes only." DaVinci explains.

"Everybody in Florence knows that, Maestro, and they are extremely disappointed.

But I also travelled here to buy the portrait back. At whatever cost his majesty demands,"

Giocondo admits. "Do you think he would consider selling it to me?"

"No," DaVinci answers simply.

"Why not?" Giocondo asks.

"Because he is The King of France," DaVinci says, "And you are The King of Pants."

Both men break into hysterical laughter until tears run down their respective faces.

"Touché, Maestro," says Giocondo. "That is French for you got me good."

"If I have offended you in any way, Mr. Giocondo, I apologize," says DaVinci.

"To be completely honest, Mr. DaVinci, "I want to apologize to you." Giocondo admits. "That is the most important reason I travelled so many days to France."

"Apologize to me. Why?" asks DaVinci.

Giocondo stands up, walks around the glass gazebo, sits back down at the table and continues his apology. "For my past, unprofessional behavior and childish disrespect."

"Never forget your arrogance and purple dye," says DaVinci, "And the mistreatment of your wife. And your condescension of her flock of Uccellisa that has raised more money for children's health than any other organization in Italy…perhaps in the world."

"Lisa absolved me of all that years ago," Giocondo says. "I hope you will, as well."

Giocondo looks through the pockets of his coat draped on the bistro chair. He locates the correct pocket, takes out a beautifully wrapped package and hands it to DaVinci.

"Could you please open that for me, Mr. Giocondo?" says DaVinci. "My right hand is now permanently not right."

Giocondo delicately unwraps the package and puts twelve

miniature Uccellisa on the table. Each bird is the color of a panel in the robe DaVinci is wearing.

Each bird is trimmed with auroserici.

Each bird is hanging on a ribbon of magenta to match the sleeves of the robe.

"Thank you, so much, Francesco," says DaVinci, finally using Giocondo's first name.

The men stare at each other, nodding their heads.

"I also have a gift that I want you and Lisa to open. At home. Together," says DaVinci.

DaVinci slowly reaches under the table.

"You're not about to ring a security bell, are you, Maestro?" teases Giocondo.

Laughing and shaking his head, DaVinci finds a flat, square package that's well padded, carefully wrapped and ready for travel. He hands it to Giocondo.

Giocondo says, "Thank you, so much, Leonardo," finally using DaVinci's first name.

Again, the men stare at each other, smiling.

"What is it?" Giocondo asks.

THE END

About the Author

ARLENE JAFFE has surprised many people. Including herself. At age five, Arlene's first written monologue was from an indignant monkey launched into space. She's come a long way since; with short plays, long plays and everything in between; plus movie treatments, scripts, scenes and song lyrics.

Even during her long and much-awarded career as an advertising creative director, Arlene continued to explore her own writer's journey with all its twists and turns. Her passion has always been discovering obscure people, places and things …then digging for any information that might exist…then turning that research on its head for the most dramatic effect.

Finally, Arlene knew it was time for less selling and more storytelling. So she became a free agent/creative consultant. The result? This is just a partial list:

Arlene's stage plays: *Anonymous*: Mary Shelley and Walter Scott argue the authenticity of her authorship. *Search And Rescue*: Three FEMA dogs sent to find survivors at the World Trade Center. *Surrounded*: One of many projects developed in BMI's Musical Theater Workshop. *The Rock Eater*: Demystification of Howard Hughes over a fifty-year time span. *North Bend*: What may have led to the killings in Newtown. *Rita Shalimar*: A big actress has big body issues. *The River Sambre*: A teenage Magritte sees his mother drown. *ElliEli*: White hot pain, deep black comedy. *Wine and Cookies*: The prophet Elijah and Santa in rehab. *Anything You Want*: A student's pivotal meeting with Norman Rockwell. *Emigrant*: How a building got soul. *The Keys*: Reverse cyborgs learn the consequences of being human. Carriers: A play with music about the 1925 diphtheria epidemic in Alaska. *King, Lou and Linnie*: A snake, a bat and a pangolin are destined for the wet market in Wuhan, China.

Arlene's screenplays: *The One In The Middle*, A WWII clairvoyant mystery. *The Separators*, a supernatural thriller. *The Legend of the Lost Intransitu*, an animated tale of glacial proportion.

As you read this, Arlene is working on something new, obscure and surprising. She is a member of The Dramatists Guild and lives in New York's Greenwich Village.

Mr. Mona Lisa is Arlene Jaffe's first novel.